Furcifer's Pride

Book One of Vade Mecum

By D.H. Dhaenens

Flammable Penguins Publishing

Table of Contents

ISBN 978-0-9956967-0-9

FLAMMABLE PENGUINS PUBLISHING
International House
24 Holborn Viaduct
CITY OF LONDON
London EC1A 2BN

www.flammablepenguins.com

For Claire, my partner in crime and so much more.
For Kirsten, Charlie and Jessica, three of the best
friends a writer could ever wish for.

Chapter 1

Furcifer startled awake from dreams filled with monkeys, magic and the challenges that came with returning from the dead.

Perhaps sleeping on the train had not been the best idea, he realised as he quickly gathered his belongings which he had heaped on the seat next to him. He had planned to review his situation and figure out what to do while on the way. But travel fatigue had caught up with him and he had put his head down and slept. Instead of arriving at least half prepared, he found himself fumbling for his ticket and thinking about where to go to next at the same time. This lead to the minor annoyance of people bumping into him, his bag sliding off of his shoulder and into his hand. Without a thought he grabbed the sliding strap and swung it back onto his shoulders. His travels in India had made him too used to crowds for this to bother him. This was minor compared to any proper market, where everyone was bustling to get where they needed to be and where the smells were sometimes overpowering and disorienting. He easily ignored the passive aggressive looks of people who wanted him to just hurry up already and get out of their way as he made his own way through the grey station halls. With a leisurely yawn he joined the queue at the ticket gate.

He slid his ticket through the reader and exited the platform. Right. Where to next? Dean Mara Terry had sent him a few letters after he had sent his research over, at first verifying it was actually him. Her concern had struck him – they had been good friends once, long ago. A distant but pleasant memory. They had spent many a coffee date together, even at this station, he realised as he took it all in. Sure, the halls had changed, but the coffee shop where they had gotten their first cup of coffee after disembarking from their commuter train together was still there. He shook his head. Maybe he could go get a cup of coffee, for old time's sake, and see if the old barista still recognised him.

But first of all – in the dean's last letter to him she had asked him to get a phone and save her number into it as soon as he could. It had also contained a pre-charged credit card which would buy a phone and some food to last him until he got to the university. He marched past the coffee shop, straight towards a small electronics kiosk and let his hands slide briefly over the counter before greeting the clerk with a single look. The clerk, a gruff man with a name tag which read Milun, just shrugged back, though he could swear he saw a glimmer of recognition. Maybe the man recognised him from when he walked through this station daily. Rather than giving it further thought, he looked back at the counter filled with phones. So much choice for a device that was only meant to do one or two things... In the end he picked out a small smartphone and a prepaid sim with enough credit to last a few calls. Being a mage did not mean he shunned technology, he just had not needed a phone the last few years.

News had come through via Dean Terry just before he had boarded the train. His house had been sold shortly after he had been declared officially dead. Of course he had noticed his funding not coming through anymore, but he'd just not gotten to chasing that up. Three years of being out of touch was barely reason to call anyone dead, he felt. Unfortunately most of the world didn't seem to agree with this point of view. His university had begrudgingly taken him back, though that grudge faded almost immediately when he could present an entire monograph on how India used magic and their views on it. Just how much it had changed their culture was quite easy to see and they were so far the only place where even animals had magic. It seemed some monkeys had developed magical powers and it was quite interesting. Studying them he had found out that they seemed to use the same hand movements to direct the magic as humans did and that they seemed to use it sparingly, only employing it in cases of danger. He had seen one levitate himself to a tree branch after a dangerous miscalculation of a jump, and another had flicked away a predator chasing him and his family. The concept of performing magic without a spell was seen as a great skill, so to know such small animals handled it quite easily was intriguing. It had been only a few years since people had come out claiming they had magic, and science and academia were still rushing to understand and bring out a coherent theory first. Perhaps that was why the university was so happy to take him back – he had magic himself, which meant first-hand knowledge. Even so, three years ago he had not just decided to run towards the place where the magic seemed to originate. He had also run away from the emerging magic scene – groups of magic users who tried to separate themselves from humans.

But none of that was important right now. Giving into nostalgia he walked to the coffee shop and ordered his usual. That would buy him some time before he would have to come to terms with the fact that he was, effectively, going to be living in a college dorm.

With a sigh he took his coffee and sat down. After spending a year with the monkeys he had sent his findings to the university, who had turned out to be very surprised to hear from him. After he had sorted out the initial confusion, he had heard from them that he had been declared legally dead, his belongings and his house were sold. The university could offer him his job back and a dorm to stay in, but that was about it. He started unpacking the phone and slid in the small sim card. At least it seemed to have some charge.

With slow and deliberate fingers, he typed up his first text message.

```
    Hi dean, just arrived. Taking the bus over
 to the university. Should arrive in about an
            hour This is Atze Furcifer.
```

He reread it silently before hitting send. A few moments later, the phone dinged, signalling the arrival of an answer

```
   Hi. Ur keys in envelop @ door of twer. MT
```

What was that supposed to mean? The man squinted at the screen, some locks of red hair falling in front of his face as he sounded it out.

"What the hell's a twer." He muttered to himself, before grinning. The tower. She had given him the tower of the university building. Ah, she'd always had a sense of humour.

With a chuckle he put the phone away and focussed on the cup of tea in front of him. What was less positive were his belongings being sold? There were some…. dubious items in there, which could get him fired. That would not look very good on his CV, considering he had only just gotten his job back after a long disappearance.

He stirred some sugar through his tea. The coffee shop sounds, mixed with the sound of chatter and espresso machines, put him on edge, making him realise just how long he had been away for. It would take a while to get used to civilisation again - or at least the urban jungle he found himself in.

He noticed he had been clutching the cookie that came with his tea - a habit to keep monkeys from running off with the treat. With a chuckle he let go and sipped the tea.

Nothing had changed. People rushed to trains - though the boards looked a little newer and there were other shops than the last time he had come through here. The tea was still good. He stirred it absently and looked around, trying to remember when he had been to the station last. It didn't matter much. Time had passed and that was basically all.

Nothing had changed for him here. Last he checked it was still illegal for him to use university funded research in publicly published books. But as time passed and more magic emerged, more and more people found themselves with strange new powers that they could not control. He was one of the few who had even an inkling about how it worked. He couldn't keep it from people just because the university wanted to wait and produce a very small and very exclusive run of expensive teaching books, only available to a few professors, with the work he had done. As far as he cared, his work was his own. Perhaps he would be able to renegotiate his contract now that he was rehired... Put a clause in that he could publish works outside of the university.

Back when he had taken the job it had seemed like the best deal ever. He wouldn't have to deal with publishers and writing very much, and they paid for everything else, leaving him free to go and explore this whole new world.

A decade of research had left his view less rosy. The university didn't want to help people, they wanted to help paying students and old professors who misread everything he wrote and then taught it the wrong way. And even then – there was talk of dropping the upcoming magic courses before they had even started as there was not enough interest in the specialisation.

Of course there wasn't! Maybe two percent of people were afflicted by the sudden appearance of magic, and not that many lived in a developed country like this one. There was no way of counting them, either, as people could have the power but never see it manifested. He had seen people who could manipulate time without realising – they just thought it was luck the bus had not taken off yet when they ran towards the bus stop. Or that they never seemed to be getting sick. That was the tragedy of it – people who didn't realise they had magic.

He swigged back the last sip of tea and left. Without a phone or a working internet connection since Mumbai it had been hard to arrange transport, so he would be relying on public transport. He grabbed a hold of his backpack and easily located the bus stops just outside of the station

Working at a university usually had one upside: they were easy to get to. Within minutes, he found a bus that went directly to campus and boarded it, trying to find a seat among the students. It seemed the academic year was about to start – all kinds of young people were sharing the bus with him. The front of the bus had filled up fast, but he finally found a space in the back.

It seemed he wasn't the only one who had been looking for a seat, as he saw a girl approach almost as soon as he had sat down.

"Hey. Mind if I sit here?" The brunette teenager asked, looking down at the seat taken by Furcifer's bag. She was wearing a simple dress and a cardigan with a logo he recognised pretty well - the Canutta school for girls, a gordian knot. The founders believed the myth of Gordias, the tale of an ox farmer who had driven into Telmissus shortly after the oracle of the city had declared that the next man to drive an ox cart into the city would be king. Similarly, they believed that a higher power gifted them magic, through some system that was too divine for them to predict.

He was familiar with the academy. It was a prestigious, expensive girl's only school to most people. It was, however, also one of the oldest institutions for girls with magic. It had grown from a small coven of female mages to become a network of schools, all with the knot in their shield. Last he had heard, they were actually forming a Faction - a recognised unit in the magic world that was responsible for the members it had and differentiated itself from other groups by their specific set of rules and morals.

"Uh. Sure..."

Furcifer looked around, but when he saw no other seats available, he removed his backpack from the seat. He preferred to avoid people sitting next to him, as he didn't want stares or to spend his time explaining his appearance. Magic had actually caused some physical changes in him – his black hair had turned a vivid red. His eyes had turned from a dark brown to a very light blue overnight, and his skin tone had turned evenly pale and almost translucent. Freckles were no longer an issue, but his usual resistance to the sun was also gone – most of his money in India had gone to sunscreen.

"Are you enrolling at the university as well?" Asked the girl, looking over him.

Furcifer guessed she was new in town and was trying to make friends as soon as she could to ease herself.

"Not really. I'm a researcher, slash lecturer." He held a hand out. "Atze Furcifer. You can call me Furcifer."

"Furcifer. Nice to meet you. I'm Manon Conway."

She shook his hand, relaxing a little now that she had found a seat for the way. She looked quite striking, with dark auburn hair. Though she was not as young as the other students on the bus, she had an open and honest face which he guessed was her biggest ace when making friends. Definitely someone who was part of several friend groups. Furcifer figured she had not had many friends once upon a time, which lead to her trying hard to make many of them now.

"Lovely to meet you." Furcifer said politely. "You're starting at the university then?"

"Yes." She nodded, looking out the window as the bus departed. "Master's degree for biology and art."

She straightened up, looking as if she was preparing to defend that combination.

"I think it's a good combination." Furcifer said.

Immediately, Manon relaxed. He had obviously said the right thing.

"So, you are moving into the dorms?"

"Yes." She said.

"I'm quite looking forward to it! It'll be so different from my university, like a new start. I may even join a sorority..." She chuckled at that a little. "But really, I want to go to class every day and - the sorority girls might be able to help with notes and studying."

Furcifer nodded. He'd often heard the story - and then they usually would spend days partying and only studying the day before the exam.

"Just stay focussed. Also, I need to move into the dorms as well... So I might be able to show you around a bit." He said, looking over to her.

As he thought about it, he could use a friend as much as the girl next to him could. Someone to keep him grounded and someone who would come looking for him if he hadn't been out of his room in five days. Someone who... would be a friend, he guessed. With a sigh he sat back and closed his eyes.

"Just wake me up when we get to the university, okay?" He asked.

"Hey, wake up!"

Manon gave him a poke when they got to the university. It had apparently been a very short drive as she had not relaxed whatsoever. If anything, her excitement seemed to have grown. She was peering around out the window and almost startled Furcifer with how fast she jumped up once the bus had stopped.

"Come on! I want to go check out the dorms!" She said, brushing past Furcifer and rushing out the bus.

Furcifer followed her out, almost struck with how disappointed the young woman looked with the dark, old fashioned building before them.

"Prime example of gothic architecture." Furcifer tried to cheer her up, pointing at one of the towers.

"Look. That's where they're stashing me." He grinned, quite amused by the fact that the mage had a room in a tower. There had to be some bureaucrat on the board chuckling at that.

"Uhuh." Manon raised an eyebrow. "No way you can afford that." The rooms within the building were prohibitively expensive and only rarely rented out as student accommodation, instead being used as offices for lecturers.

"Told you, I'm working for the university. They probably just gave it to me as it's the cheapest option." He shrugged. He didn't imagine they were jumping to let him stay in an expensive room after all that had happened. Or would want to let him out of their sight.

"I'll be seeing you around."

He left the woman, who seemed to regain her happy mood as she grabbed her bag and looked around. A few other students were finding their way around, so she just started following one group. As she started talking to another student, Furcifer turned around and walked into the building. Almost immediately he stumbled over a bucket full of water, kicking it over, only barely keeping himself from falling over. His feet, however, were soaked.

"Excuse me!" The cleaning lady swabbed at the ground near his feet. "Watch where you're going!"

"Well I never."

He muttered and made a face at her, though he instantly regretted that as he felt the mop slap against his lower legs. Deciding it unwise to take this little exchange further, he hurried onwards, pant legs sticking to his wet legs.

As he proceeded into the hall, he took a deep breath of the cool air inside. Despite large amounts of people and computers, the air was always chilly and fresh in here – possibly a feature of the antique architecture. He definitely felt the cold on his wet shins. The floors were tiled in old fashioned tiles, chipped cream and brown mosaic, and depicted fleurs de lis and chalices. The walls separating the halls from the outside world had large arch shaped glass panels in them, the tops of which were decorated with stained glass through which the sunlight played. Most of it seemed to go unnoticed by the people passing through the halls, though they were mostly students rushing to another building or to an orientation session. Classes would start in a week or so, but the freshmen were already present to buy books and be shown around by others.

Furcifer walked through the halls, which felt a little like home to him. He had started his studies here and had achieved two degrees before becoming a researcher and a professor, teaching courses in philosophy and research techniques. His courses were popular, and while he was not the best professor, he was kind, patient and caring. His students felt like he cared whether they passed or failed and did their best to pass his courses.

His old life, he would call it. He had lived a few miles from here, walked to work in his lovely little suit, and taught his class. He had actually enjoyed teaching, especially as many of his courses allowed him to do research with his students.

It had literally changed overnight. His magic powers were not even the first thing he had noticed. He'd woken up with red hair, this pale skin and eyes which were so unusual. Even his temper had changed - he was no longer patient and caring, but found himself to be more sarcastic and short- tempered. In addition to his looks drawing unwanted attention, his classes became less and less popular as he became known as that asshole teacher who would yell at the slower students.

Like he cared, he would tell himself as he saw the registration count drop. Slowly but surely, he was pulled behind the scenes to do more research and less teaching.

This seemed to be where he excelled. After a while he had found himself again and became a happier person for it. Or at least a better one. He could stand being alone for much longer amounts of time than before. He could also focus longer on details other people wrote off as anomalies.

He had started researching magic alongside metaphysical philosophy, being one of the first to actually study this new-fangled 'magic' phenomenon. There had been no experts on magic, nor had anyone even tried to figure out why it suddenly sprang into existence in a world filled with technology. And to be honest many found the idea a bit silly - there was no such thing as magic. Magic happened in stories.

In a lot of ways, magic was useless. A lot of its effects could be reproduced with a machine, and often it was easier to build a machine than to do it with magic. This had intrigued Furcifer. There were manuals to build machines, so why wouldn't there be manuals for magic?

Of course, he was still working for the university, so any research he did on the subject belonged to them. To get it out there he had started publishing it covertly, without permission and without attaching his real name. Distributing the books like zines, making sure that they were out there for the ones who needed them.

The ding of the elevator got Furcifer out of his train of thought. He looked up at the opening doors and slipped in smoothly, pushing the top button without paying attention to anyone else. The largest part of his luggage had gone missing half way to Bangkok, so he had ordered new clothes, a few necessities and some groceries to be delivered the next day using the wifi at the station. While he lived for magic, he could not see himself living without technology. With a little smile at that thought, he started looking up at the display above the door, eager to reach his room.

Chapter 2

Furcifer opened up the last box of books that had been sent over to the small room. Settling in was easier than he had imagined. Over the next few days the deliveries came in, creating a bit of breathing space as he set his living space up. The hoodie he'd been wearing for the last week now resided in a plastic bag, ready to go to the laundromat with a few other things, and he had set up his laptop on the desk.

Bookshelves lined the wall of the semi-circular bedroom. In the circular part, he had set up a bed and some smaller bookshelves, basically just for the books he was using that week. It had little room for other luxuries. His small bedroom connected to a slightly larger living space with a hob and sink, where he had set up a large down trodden couch which served as a space to sit and eat. Furcifer didn't understand the concept of a dining room as he did not believe in stopping all activities just to have a meal.

Furcifer quickly counted the books before unwrapping the last book from the layers of tissue paper. It was his oldest book and always the first to be packed. Between the brown leather covers was a wealth of information gathered by a man named A. Ward who had seen magic emerge in the early seventeenth century. It was a compelling read and his greatest treasure. Gingerly, he flicked through the brittle pages until he found his favourite passage.

The young lady found herself poorly and did not partake in the celebrations of that night. Milun and myself made sure to bring her home and promised her mother, a family friend, that we would look out for her. We happily accepted as her homestead was close to the large woods, near the edge where many herbs grow wild in the bright sunlight. Overnight we took turns in watching the girl and collecting herbs. During one of my watches, the young woman suddenly tossed and turned and a change came over her. Her hair and skin darkened until she was left with grey skin and strange green tinted hair. Both of us sensed a deeper change in her, however, finding that she now had a ready and keen sense of magic.

He closed the book as the writer continued theorizing about the reason for that change and the sudden appearance of magic in his home town. This was the earliest account he had found about such a sudden appearance change and the birth of magic within a person, which made it very important to him. Of all the people who matured into magic, only few had such a dramatic change of appearance. In fact, in the current time, he only knew one other who had had such a transformation. It was still a mystery. With a contemplative sigh, he walked over to the shelf to carefully fit the book in.

Thankfully, most of his books had survived the trip back. One or two had gone missing, but they were replaceable. Irreplaceable, however, were the books he had left at his house before going on his adventure.

They were not so much books as his own notes, almost manuscripts to the spell books he published. Unlike the published books, these writings did trace back to him. From spells he had invented to receipts from the university cafe, stupidly used as bookmarks, the book would easily spill the identity of its author. His only saving grace was that he hoped people would assume it was just the notebook of a deluded man and not do too much digging into the origins of it.

Best case, it was out there in a storage area. Worst case, it was in the hands of campus lawyers already, and he had been lured back here to be confronted with his trespasses. Furcifer had been paranoid the first day or so, but there had been no sign of anyone following him or even scrutinising his actions much.

In fact the only attention he had received was a request from the dean to set up a curriculum for the magic courses, and she had offered to let him teach it. Part of him was disappointed that this smartphone thing meant she could reach him anywhere and he had no excuse to not read his emails, but he was flattered by the offer. He'd only been back for a few days and hadn't even been able to present any findings, though the dean had implied he could use his latest research in his curriculum.

Well, that would be hard to do if he didn't write it down first, he thought with a chuckle. His notebooks formed semi-coherent texts, written in spurs of the moments, where he had just had a bright idea or had seen someone do something interesting. To boil them down into lessons would be hard.

He grabbed his messenger bag and a few books and climbed down the stairs to the cafeteria in the main hall. Planning a curriculum gave him a reason to look busy while he tracked down his books, at least. Being a staff member meant he could get his meals for free, a privilege he happily abused. He had tried his hand at home cooking but found the room easily filled up with the cooking smell and it was hardly impossible to use the small old kitchen without triggering the fire detector. So ramen or cooking spaghetti? Fine. Actual cooking that required two or more hobs at the same time? Quite dangerous and possibly ending up in a visit from the fire warden to make sure nothing was on fire.

Furcifer grabbed a garden salad and flashed his badge at the cashier. She just gave him a look and shrugged - everyone knew the scary looking man with the shocking red hair and light skin. Furcifer winked at her and went to sit in a distant corner, away from most people. Only the hum of the tray conveyor belt which transported trays into the kitchen was audible from here and it was strangely soothing to Furcifer, who grew nervous when everything was quiet. As he sat down he started to block out the noise, and opened one of the books he had brought down with him in his messenger bag.

Hidden in his books were letters. He had gotten to know a lot of other mage over time, and he had reached out to them to try and find his books again. So far he'd had little luck, but the last batch of letters had turned up some results. An old friend from his college days, Karen, remembered seeing the red-covered books in a charity shop, priced at some exorbitant amount which put them out of her price range. She had not been able to refrain from joking that she thought it was rather overpriced for Furcifer's scribbles.

Furcifer sighed and closed the book with the letter inside. Money would be an obstacle. As in he didn't have any. The university only paid him a stipend as he was mostly paid in benefits like free housing and free food. Truth be told he had preferred the benefits over the extra cash as it meant he didn't have to worry about such petty things as grocery shopping and rent, but it left him at a bit of a disadvantage now. The longer he waited, the more chance there was someone actually bought the books he was trying to reclaim.

Furcifer poked at his salad as he contemplated his options.

Legitimate ways to retrieve the books seemed easy enough. Get a loan or an advance on his paychecks and buy the books. The exorbitant price mentioned in the letter, however, meant it would need to be at least three months' worth of salary.

He could always try and claim them back as being the rightful owner, but that meant that if the books had been identified by the university lawyers, he would pretty much be confessing on the spot. The university had not given him these funds to freely publish his findings No, buying them would be the safest approach. What could be more natural than a mage curious about some magic scribbles in a mysterious book?

Money, however, would be the main issue with that approach. If he asked the university to pay for the purchase they would be interested in what was in them, and that could not happen.

He could steal them. That would be easy enough with some magic and a bit of planning, but it relied on too many variables. If the book was stashed in a glass case, or had been moved to another store, he would need to plan all over again. A failed attempt to steal the books could also warn the shop owner that the book was worth stealing and should be looked at a little more closely.

This was a pickle. No matter what he did it would require a well-considered approach and a clear head. There could be no distractions if he wanted to pull this off in a discreet manner. Not to mention, the dean had also asked him to go look at an item in the local museum. Apparently it had made one curator sick, and the staff swore that it was haunted... or something. Even the dean knew that items, much like people, could have intrinsic magic. They had had long conversations on the subject after he had gained his own powers, even if those conversations now seemed horribly silly and uneducated. He'd had no idea back then about anything.

Suddenly there was a flurry of movement in front of him as someone quickly sat down on the seat across from him. As he looked up to tell them off for just grabbing the seat without asking, he saw Manon, smiling brightly. She put down a tray filled with a burger, two portions of chips and a milkshake.

"Hey! Fancy seeing you around here, the tower doesn't have a Michelin restaurant built into it?"

"Can't even cook an egg up there without triggering a fire alarm." Furcifer looked over the girl.

College life seemed to become her - she looked chipper and well-rested.

"I'm guessing they need to be careful up there."

Nodded Manon gravely as she picked up her fork, before realising she would not need it and just grabbing the burger with her two hands.

"Wouldn't be the first time that part of the building caught fire. Hey, did you know you run a really big risk of being hit by lightning?" She said between big bites of the burger.

"Comforting." Furcifer looked down at his plate and speared some leaves of lettuce. He tried hard to feign interest in the girl.

"How is the settling in going?" He asked. Though she distracted him from his thoughts, he had to admit it was a nice change of pace to talk to someone who was not his boss.

"I think it's going well. Making friends. Roommate is ok." The student shrugged. "I... miss home though."

"I bet it must be different here, with so few people having magic." He ventured, guessing the cause of her homesickness.

"How did you – "She whispered and peered around. "The Canutta School prides itself on its discretion!"

"You wore a cardigan with your school logo when we met. In fact, isn't that hoodie...." He raised an eyebrow as she quickly checked it and groaned. Her hoodie indeed had the Canutta school logo on it.

"Listen, I only know because... I have magic myself." He conceded. No use being mean to the girl. "I'm not with any group, I've only realised I'm magic a few years ago."

She nodded gravely.

"That makes sense... my whole family got it a few years ago." She took a deep breath.

"So, you're also –"

"Tell you what. I'm teaching a course on magic this semester. It's a master's level elective..." Furcifer continued. "You should come." He finished the salad and wiped his mouth.

"Wait... you're teaching...?" The girl raised an eyebrow, still not making much sense of any of this.

"Yes, I am teaching, because I am a magic researcher and I was teaching here before magic had surfaced. You need my resume or something?" He raised an eyebrow and flicked a finger in the air, flipping his empty plate upside down. Manon jumped a little to avoid the sudden splash of leftover dressing.

"If you, as you say, have magic, you'll be an addition to a class which will mostly be non-mages. So I would like for you to join. Your insights as a student of magic will be valuable." He insisted, turning plate up right again after a glare from one of the cleaners roaming around the cafeteria. He glared back to the cleaner, but the angry look he got back made him cringe.

Manon chuckled at the small exchange...

"What, you two have a history?"

"Middle aged rage with a mop..." He muttered, before wiping his hand over the table, instantly cleaning it of all sauce without leaving a trace on his hand.

Manon's face lit up. Furcifer guessed this was the first time she had seen magic outside of her sheltered little world, and it only made him further realise that he needed to do this. After he got his books back he would be able to set up a syllabus and make up some kind of course structure that would be inclusive of non-magic users.

Furcifer got up and stacked his dirty dish and trash onto the tray. He still had to go to the museum to appraise the item and it was already getting late.

"I must get going, I am needed on an important mission. Something with the museum. I fell asleep when she mentioned Public Relations. If you want to practice some magic before class, come find me in the tower." She probably missed practicing, but her faction did not allow public use of magic.

Crap. If he was not careful he would start to enjoy human company again. Somewhere along the way he seemed to have forgotten that he wasn't the only one with magic. That there were other people out there he was doing all this for.

...

Chapter 3

Even as the light of the setting sun warmed the appearance of the cold walls, Furcifer had imagined the back halls of the museum to be more... ornate. Older and more stylish. In reality they were dark grey, large bricked walls with quite basic lighting and security doors. From the looks of it, it could easily withstand fires and burglars. And when you were guarding treasures, Furcifer guessed that is what you would want in your security over decorum.

The assistant fumbled with his keys, and Furcifer did his best to ignore him in order to not make him more nervous. He was supposed to meet the director and then see this suspected magical artefact that had turned up. However, the lady at the desk had seemed unaware about an appointment, so she had grabbed an intern to lead him to the director's office.

Furcifer was not expecting to be impressed. At best, these suspected magical artefacts had some sort of electromagnetic field. They tended to induce vibrations, sounds and other creepy things, but these phenomena were not at all related to magic. At the worst he'd be looking at some boring log and pretend to be interested while the director bragged on about its recovery.

Finally, the assistant found the right key and pushed the door open with a triumphant grin.

Furcifer just faked a smile and walked on with him. He just really wanted to see this item and get on with it.

They arrived at their destination quite fast after that, their footsteps echoing through the halls as they moved from the halls into the office spaces beyond and into a small waiting room. The intern walked him over to a polished looking secretary. Possibly the director's nephew, as the boy looked to be fresh out of grad school and was not even close to being as nervous as the intern before him. He had the air of a man who knew his job was both cosy and safe. And from the look of his finely tailored suit, well paid.

"Mr Donnovan will see you in ten minutes." He announced without looking up from the National Geographic he had been paging through.

Furcifer took a deep breath.

"Good. I was worried I'd be late." He said airily, giving the assistant a final look before the intern scooted off. Probably overloaded with work, Furcifer thought sympathetically. It didn't make him feel worse for treating him so coldly.

After a few minutes, the secretary stood up and opened a door for him, nodding to it sideways.

Furcifer arched a brow and pretended not to get what he was trying to communicate.

He clicked his tongue and brought his heels together.

"Mr Donnovan has found a slot for you, sir."

"Ah, thank you!" Furcifer said, getting up. "Do I tip you, or...?"

His eyes shot fire at him, making him decide to hurry up and get into the office.

At least the office was better decorated. The air in here was definitely more homely, warmer. The wallpaper and carpet were beautiful and matched in colour. The director had obviously used his own funds for this room, which gave Furcifer a hint just how much of his time the man must spend in here. The tiffany lamp was definitely not in the museum budget.

Donnovan did not even look up as the man entered the room, writing away on a thick pad of cream coloured paper. The Montblanc Meisterstück scratching softly on the paper was the only sound audible in the roomy office.

Furcifer stayed standing long enough to be polite, then sat down across from the director. While he himself was not very pleasant, he tried to make an effort when he was sent out for university business. After all, he was representing the university. Also, it was possible they would not bail him out if he did go too far.

"Mr...Furcifer." Donnovan looked up. Mid-fifties, well groomed, indented ring finger.

Furcifer smiled. "Mr Donnovan. Thank you for making time for me." His smile was hardly any more sincere than the one he had shown the intern, but it seemed to fool the man in front of him.

"Not at all! My pleasure, my pleasure. The Museum of Natural History loves to be on the forefront of modern society, showing how history and the future are just... stages. We consider this new development of magic to be of the utmost importance. There are many people out there shying away from this, but we enjoy being on the edge, to discover like the explorers who brought us our first artefacts over a century ago -"

Furcifer just let him talk until he found a point to intervene.

"So you mentioned this artefact?" He sat up a bit straighter.

Even checking out a fake would be a lot more fun than sitting here, listening to the man brag about how much better he had made the museum.

Donnovan blinked, having been interrupted in his speech.

"Ah yes. Of course. I wouldn't want to waste any of your precious time."

Furcifer was sure he tasted some sour in those words. Perhaps he could grow to like the man.

The artefact sat in the middle of the adjacent room, displayed on a red velvety stand under a glass case. While it definitely looked magical it didn't feel that way to Furcifer. He had to resist the urge to sigh deeply - he would still have to play at inspecting it, looking it over and giving his "honest opinion" on the piece. The faster he did that the faster he could be out of here. He took a deep breath as the director made a big show of slipping on a pair of cotton gloves before he picked up the item.

From up close, it looked like a simple bangle. It seemed to be three pieces of gold wire, fishtail braided together. Definitely old, definitely valuable. Magic? No real sign of it.

"So Mr Donnovan. Can I just ask when you found this item?" He asked, stretching time a bit. The university was paid by the hour for the visit so he might as well try and round it up to one hour at least.

"Just a few years ago." The director cleared his throat, obviously not used to answering questions as if he was a simple curator or something equally silly.

That was quite recent, Furcifer pondered.

"It seems Roman in origin?" Furcifer guessed, never been one to study the art side of history very much. It looked old enough to be Roman and the braiding technique was very typical.

"Seems, yes. But it is actually an Edwardian piece, probably made to resemble a Roman piece." The director had to go and pick up a file to give that information.

Furcifer straightened up. Someone had made those notes in that file – that would be the person to speak to. The person who loved this piece, studied it, no matter what it was supposed to be. Not the fame hungry director trying to sell a future attraction.

Furcifer gave a nod and looked at the file. "Who has been curating the piece?"

"Oh.... A young curator. We uh, had to let him go."

Furcifer raised an eyebrow. "May I ask why exactly?"

"He was... a little disturbed. Believed the piece belonged to him and that he was chosen to protect it with his life."

The director seemed unwilling to say much more about it, which Furcifer thought was a good sign.

"But... When the magic properties were noted, the uh, piece was being... handled by him." The director cleared his throat and made a disapproving face.

"Without gloves I'm assuming?" He guessed from the man's reaction.

"You would assume correctly." The man cleared his throat. "We let him go after he tried to steal the item."

"Why did you let him handle it without gloves?" Furcifer insisted.

"It is poor form. But junior curators will often forget to use them in the early stages, as a lot of items we get turn out to be worthless. We do crack down on it and instruct all curators to use gloves, but I have caught Jeffrey not using any from time to time."

Interesting. A so called magical item which lay idle, pretending to be a normal, day to day ordinary bangle, until it was touched by the right person.

Magic's resurgence was new and still not widely accepted. The best way to hide a magical artefact would be exactly such an enchantment. But the person who made the enchantment would not behave so stupidly around the item... Unless the person who had curated it was simply affected by it.

There was a theory out there, that some people had higher magical defences than others. However, it was hard to study when so few people had come forward with powers. Perhaps Jeffrey's defences were simply too low for such an item, whereas an ordinary person would not even notice the bangle was anything special.

Perhaps the bangle was looking for a new owner. Furcifer looked over the item then glanced at the curator.

"To tell you the truth... I can't say much about this item just yet. From what you told me it just might be..." He tapped his chin. "Would it be possible to go see this curator?"

The best way now was to convince this man that perhaps the item actually was magic. To keep him engaged in this. Plant the little thought that perhaps there was something to it worth pursuing. It would make the man eager to help. And right now, Furcifer needed his help. He looked up from the bangle to the director. He looked a little exasperated. Good.

"Alright. I will give you his address, but please be... discreet." He insisted.

"Of course. But I cannot miss the opportunity to get to know this artefact more. The university would be thrilled to sponsor the exhibition of a magical item. Between us.... The university has asked me to prepare a course on magic. This would be the perfect exhibition to go along with that. You know, promoting our own new courses, generate interest in magic. Many young visitors coming over..." He buttered up the man shamelessly. His own fault for making his motivation so blatantly clear.

The director's eyes twinkled a moment as he handed over the file.

"His address and findings are in here."

At that moment, Furcifer was sure he could have asked for his daughter's hand in marriage and have the man consented. For now, however, the file was enough.

Chapter 4

Furcifer left the museum a few hours later. He had taken advantage of the free entrance ticket to browse the other exhibitions which the museum had on show, just to make sure there were no other rogue magical items, of course.

While interesting, there had been nothing. It was strange that even in the boxes filled with other items acquired around the same time and in the same area as the bangle, none of them had any magic whatsoever. It was basically tat, probably from some Moroccan market, hastily bought to cover up a lack of actual archaeological finds. While these markets did sometimes have illegitimate items which had been stolen from digs, usually they were cheap silver crafts.

In that way, the bangle stood out. It was simple and almost... boring. On its own, it wouldn't stand out on a market stall filled with exotic items, fake or real. If you were to pick out something to pass off as an antique artefact, surely one would choose something a little flashier.

But for now, he had done enough sleuthing. Furcifer took out his phone and reviewed the emails he had received about his notebook. It had been spotted in a charity shop nearby, which meant he would definitely have to check it out. With a few touches he mapped out a route to the charity shop in question.

Furcifer hadn't been in a charity shop for ages. They were once his favourite haunt, perfect for his thrifty personality and picky tastes. These stores had masses of cheap books, clothes which were pretty much wearable, sometimes even the occasional bed spread that would stop smelling of old person after three or four washes.

There was something magical about these shops. They contained an amalgamation of items that nobody had chosen to put together but still formed a coherent theme as old fashioned porcelain dolls were posed next to a beanie baby. A worn puzzle next to a game of Monopoly which used credit cards. And every time he went in there he discovered new things.

Books were his favourites. The old volunteer ladies were rigid in what they did or did not accept, so only books in good condition were accepted. He couldn't imagine how many books were discarded that way, but it at least kept the hygiene levels in the store acceptable. Another advantage was that they weren't always printed books.

Furcifer found himself falling back into old shopping habits. He just barely looked over the books, at first not spotting the notebook. That was alright, he would find it. He browsed the clothes briefly then returned to the books. His stomach sunk somewhat – there was no note book here.

"Excuse me." He walked up to a volunteer. "Is that all of your books?"

The volunteer lady looked up. "No, not the only ones. But the ones we have for sale right now."

"I'm looking for a red notebook."

"We have a few of those in our new items section." She briefly pointed a pen at a rack of cheap, off brand notebooks.

"No no no. Not like that. A red ringed notebook that had been written in."

Her face lit up a little. "Yes! We did have one. I sold it to a nice young man." She nodded.

"With a discount, because he helped out here before. He's such a darling, changing lightbulbs for us... "

Furcifer's head fell back and he groaned. "Alright. Could have led with that, but hey."

He sighed. There was no use asking her who it was sold to – if anything that would seem shifty. Secondly, even if he did a truth spell on her – she was older and more resilient to it. People who had gone through many different experiences in their lifetime had often more of a tolerance. It was a form of manipulation, much like lying – hard to do and easy to spot. And people didn't like it when they caught you doing it. Worst of all, it was not reliable at all. If the user could not tell a liar from someone speaking the truth, it was hard to tell if it even worked.

He had left the store in a bit of a mood, and had decided he should go ahead and finish his work for the day. It would be useless to go home with what little he had on the bangle right now anyway. With no further clues on the notebook's whereabouts beyond "a nice young man", it would take a while to find it, if he ever did. The fact it had been bought was scary. What if the owner found out what it really was?

The apartment building was rather new and simple in its layout. A row of mailboxes flanked him as he walked in. As he took the elevator up to the sixth floor, Furcifer checked the flat number in his notes. He reached the correct floor and knocked at the door of flat 19, looking around as he waited. The floor was the same boring brown tile as the ground floor had had, and there were about five flats per floor. As the neighbour across the way walked out to walk her dog, a waft of cooking smells greeted him.

On his way over he had done some research on the man. The usual web searching – scouring his LinkedIn, articles he had worked on, social media. It was all pretty standard. City boy who had gone to the city university for a degree in literature and management. He had added a degree in art history as well. After that he had gone to work for the museum almost straight away, and had been there until he had been dismissed.

He walked up to flat 19 and knocked rapidly. When the door opened, Furcifer frowned. He had seen pictures of Jeffrey during his web browsing. He had looked like a jolly, chubby man with dark hair, not this scrawny Scandinavian standing in front of him.

"I'm looking for... Jeffrey... Stone?" He read off a shred off of a notebook.

He noticed a name tag, a light blue Pet World one, identifying the blond as "Assistant manager Russell Marson". He didn't even look like an assistant manager. The man looked about twenty, with blond curls and blue eyes. A very everyday kind of face with nice cheekbones, he looked friendly and honest. Furcifer guessed he at least had that going for him.

Russell opened the door a bit wider and took a step back.

"That's my flat mate. Hang on. Jeffrey! It's uh, for you..." He said, retreating back into the flat which boasted a very open style, with the lounge visible from the door and the kitchen behind a half high wall. To the right from the entrance he could see more doors - possibly to the bedroom and bathrooms. There were some cheery decorations on the brightly painted walls, but they contrasted deeply with the sad brown tiling on the floor.

Jeffrey got up from the couch and scratched his bum as he walked up.

Furcifer was not impressed. The t-shirt he was wearing was much too loose on him, and the end of his belt was hanging out from under his t-shirt. He looked worn in the face, and the blue eyes might have had a sparkle once. Now, he just looked like a worn old man, a far cry from the jolly chubster in the picture.

"Yes?" He asked, looking over the stranger. "Oh. Are you the academic that the director said would be coming around? Come inside." He motioned towards the couch.

Furcifer sighed. He hated that term, academic. As if he did nothing but study his books all day! And this one didn't look like the academic he had expected either, but he would have to make do. He shook his head and kept in mind that Jeffrey had gotten an advance call from the director. He would have to be aware that the man had had time to prepare a story, even if his lax attitude did not suggest that. As Jeffrey walked back into the lounge, he could not resist scratching his back briefly, forcing Furcifer to suppress a groan. He wasn't so much disgusted with the man's bodily habits as with the mundane nature of it all. Where were the evil masterminds he could be outwitting? The powerful archmages? Anything would be more fun than Assistant Manager Forgettable Name and Previous Curator Number Three. Suppressing his distaste, he walked into the flat and followed Jeffrey back to the couch. Russell was still hanging around the room, seemingly worried about Jeffrey. He was pretending to be busy cleaning up a little, but Furcifer could tell he was merely pushing stuff around rather than really tidying up

"My name is Furcifer. I'm the researcher who would be coming around to ask what you know about this bangle." He crossed his arms and looked over to him. "Your director seems to think it's magical."

"Figures." He sighed and sank down onto the couch, motioning for Furcifer to sit down as well.

Furcifer accepted the seat and looked around.

The lounge was nicely designed. A very nice deep piled rug, a nice modern Ikea couch and a modern glass TV stand. Which made the ornate red notebook he knew so well stand out even more. Was Jeffrey the nice young man who had bought it from the charity shop? Realising what he saw, he spied around carefully. Had Jeffrey found it? That would mean he would know more about magic than the average joe out there. Had he picked it up in an attempt to understand the bangle?

What a coincidence, Furcifer thought. What were the odds? He hoped that he could play it right and walk out of here with his notebook and some extra information about the artefact.

He broke the train of thought he was getting lost in and focussed on Jeffrey.

"The director said you were very good with it." He placated the man with a little smile then got out a pen and pad. "What did you make of it? General, first impressions?" He asked. If he could get the man talking about it would be a great start. Generally with these types you just needed to get them talking, he had found.

Jeffrey groaned and looked over. "I signed a nondisclosure agreement with the museum about the terms of my leaving, so I can only tell you a bit." he sighed and looked over.

"I know." Furcifer smiled a little. "Look. None of this is going to the press. None of this will be published. If you don't want to, I can even let you read and censor my report before it goes back to the museum. I'm just... working as a consultant for the museum. Don't worry about the NDA." Right now getting the information from this man was more important than anything.

Jeffrey nodded with a sigh, obviously a little more at ease with those terms laid out for him.

"So we found the item..." Jeffrey started his story. From the discovery of the artefact, to its journey to the museum, and their findings while they had observed it at the museum. It ended up being a long story but he seemed happy he had been able to tell it.

Furcifer pretended to make some notes, though little of it was actually of interest to him. He could do without the shipping details, as he was more interested in the effect it was rumoured to have on this person. But it seemed the man was considering his career over telling a story.

Furcifer closed his notepad and nodded. "Thank you for that. So... What do you think about the director's claims?" He asked as he slid the small notepad back into his messenger bag.

"You mean, do I believe it's a magical bangle?" Jeffrey wiggled his fingers. "No, I – "

Furcifer wiggled his fingers back as if joking, but it really just sent a spell at Jeffrey to tell the truth. This was really pushing it – he had barely mastered the spell. While it would usually last a while when done properly, he hoped this one would last a minute or two.

"–I do believe there's something about it. Something scary but awesome at the same time. I am... connected to it." Droned Jeffrey, which was closer to what Furcifer wanted to hear. The mage grinned and made some notes.

"So you think it is magic." Furcifer decided.

"Yes, that's what I think indeed. I want it. I want to feel it on my skin and hold - wait, what did you do?" Hissed Jeffrey as the spell wore off.

Less than a minute, but he'd gotten what he wanted.

"Just a little truth spell." Furcifer got up and stretched out. "Now there's something else I need to retrieve...My red notebook."

"A truth spell?" Gasped Jeffrey. "That's - you can't just do that to people!"

Russell groaned. "I honestly bought it, it's mine."

He picked up the red notebook and took a step back. "And don't you dare try some Rohypnol thing on me with those freaky eyes! I'm watching you!" He made a gesture with two fingers from his own eyes to Furcifer, not sure how to deal with the fact he had just seen a man spill the honest truth after some finger waggling.

"But it was mine before it was sent to that useless shop you picked it up."

Russell held it up. "If you want it back, I want some information." He insisted, holding the book just out of reach of the mage's grabby hands.

Furcifer raised an eyebrow. "You cannot - Are you... You're blackmailing me?" He was vaguely interested in this turn of events. The man had more spunk than he could have imagined.

"Yes." Russell nodded, looking more confident now that the man seemed to be willing to talk a bit about this.

"What do you want to know?" Wondered Furcifer, cocking his head to the side a little.

"Well…" Russell took a deep breath and paged through the book a little, frowning. "Alright, first of all, what is all this?" He asked, looking up from the book briefly. It seemed he was trying to take it all in.

"A book of spells." Sighed Furcifer. "I'm technically not allowed to publish it, so be happy you weren't caught with it."

Russell gulped as he looked back at the pages. Perhaps it was better to give the book back. He held it out to the man, before holding it up again briefly.

"One more thing. Who's the girl on the first page?"

Furcifer took a deep breath. "She's just someone I keep… Seeing." He shrugged and took the book. "Thank you." He nodded and put the book away in his bag. "I should get going. Thank you for all of this." He looked to the two men.

"Alright, time to go, I'd say." Russell opened the door and ushered Furcifer out.

Furcifer winked and made his way out. "And thank you for the information… Jeffrey. I'm sure the artefact is actually magic. I will find a way to prove it."

Jeffrey groaned. "I really don't care anymore. My new job finally makes sense." He shrugged. Furcifer chuckled and made his way out to the hallway and back towards his tower.

Chapter 5

Furcifer spent the next few days going through the quite extensive notes of the former curator. When and where it was found, how and why it came to the museum, ideas to use it in an "Edwardian party" themed exhibition, which Furcifer thought was a stupid idea. Edwardians didn't party.

The notes had started out beautifully organised: dated entries into the journal, with receipts and copies of everything that had been done attached. Even the little delivery note from when the item was delivered to the museum was attached to the first page. The later pages were less neat though – it started looking as if he had been writing standing up as the writing was a lot more irregular and more imprinted into the page, as if he had pushed down hard on his pen. Where the earlier notes had neatly chronicled every moment spent on the item, the notes at the end were sporadic, vague.

"Cleaned item. It's shiny now." One entry simply read.

Another read "Boss came down."

It was a miracle the man had kept his job as long as he did, based on these notes. The bangle definitely had had some effect on him – the notes towards the end tended to become more scrawled, chaotic. One hastily attached note simply read: "Keep it away". At the end the man had suggested locking the item away in the archives. Unfortunately for him, nobody heeded that suggestion.

Poor guy, thought Furcifer, closing the book. He had now read all the notes on the artefact and he reluctantly had to admit that there was something about it. Whether it was actual magic, he could not say just yet. It had definitely had an effect on him. Perhaps the item was just coated in some sort of hallucinogenic substance.

"Suggest chemical testing of item." He noted down. The findings had pegged the bangle as an Edwardian copy of a Roman piece of jewellery, but it still would have been made in some kind of workshop. Jewellers used different mixtures of silvers and other metals, and to have an idea of what was used for this one would allow them to compare it to other items made in that era and find which jeweller had made it.

The notebook he wrote in right now was small and blue, with a university logo – his "work" notebook. It was smaller and less intimidating than his large red ledger, he had found, and a lot easier to haul along. Besides, after almost losing his latest notebook he was not going to risk taking it with him.

He put the notebook aside and took a deep breath before unlocking the desk drawer. Out came the large red ledger.

It was Friday. His course was due to start on Monday. He had better get started writing out

A crude outline for his class. Usually the outlines for courses had to be submitted much earlier, but he had been an exception to the rule as he had only arrived back recently. For now he knew no better than to use the findings from India. Magic was a complex thing. There had been mentions of magic being centuries old, but these accounts were difficult to study. They could label anything as magic, from a hairless bear to a woman with knowledge of herbs. It was best to stay with his own observations and to see the recent appearance of magic as the easiest one to study as it was still going on. Perhaps the medieval texts did describe features of magic, but it would be more productive to focus on the recent emergence of magic. Also it would be foolish to ignore the current wave of magic.

It was also the one he was the most personally invested in. When he had woken up with this new hair and new skin, it had been... disorienting to say the least. He had seen doctors, specialists, but he was physically healthy and none could reliably tell him why he had changed so much overnight. The sudden shift in personality did not make it easier at all. People he had been friends with were suddenly avoiding him and he could no longer stand to be out and socialise for more than a few hours at a time. Ironically, the biggest change had not been obvious right away. For now, though, he needed to focus on his lesson plan.

First class, you had to get their attention, make them curious, but tell them what to expect at the same time. He turned to a new page in the blue notebook and started writing.

Mission statement: introduce students to history of magic and research methods. Encourage class discussion. Generate interest in magic research as a career. Make sure course is printed by university press or suggest using the "journals" as course books. Encourage them to make notes or they'll forget anything you say within minutes.

Class one. Course introduction. Introduce self. Give as of yet non-existent course structure. Use story of Simian magic in India to generate discussion of how magic might be found in animals, and if so only in primates or also in others, and how this would affect our world.

Class two. Short history of magic. Present articles and stories from the eighties of reported magical sights. Discuss how no magic was recorded during the nineties. Then from 2000 onward discuss scholarly work on magic (mine!).

Furcifer sighed. Two classes and already he had mentioned "discussion" twice. That would be a whole lot of talking and not by him. It could lead to students going completely overboard and taking charge of the class, which was always to be avoided. Especially early on in the semester when they knew nothing of what they were talking about yet.

Secondly, using the so called illegal journals he had published under a fake name as course books might prove controversial enough to draw students to his course, but it might also lead back to him. No, the safest course of action here might be to use his own notes and copy them for the class's needs. He had an unlimited copy pass anyway, and there would be, what, twenty people enrolling in a class as vaguely outlined as his, at post graduate level? If more people showed an interest he could probably get something printed at a decent price.

Even if he used the journals, there was no way they would be traced back to him. He sent his findings to a ghost writer, who would convert them into a book for him. The similarity in writing would thus not be an issue.

Class three. Homework: write a spell. Anticipate groans. Encourage students to find a possible magical sighting and to consider it critically. Dissect a spell phrase – first real work with magic. Use white magic only – wards, protection spells.

Class four. Grade homework, discuss spells and what makes a spell phrase a spell. Explain hand gestures when doing magic, how to use them and when to not use them.

Hand gestures... Magic was difficult in that you needed to focus it somehow. Old fashioned wizards with wands had a point of focus which was easy to aim and use. Unless you wanted to walk around with a knobby dildo, however, Furcifer preferred the use of hands. It had taken him quite a while to master that, and to teach a class of beginners how to do it would be... challenging. However, not as challenging as getting students to find a wand of some sort. He sighed and looked at his own hands, bony and pale, before rubbing the cold fingers. Stay focussed.

Class five: pop quiz on spell grammar. Homework again, write three theoretical spells with description, spell phrase and aiming gestures. Go deeper into what is known about power of magic and effects of it on human beings.

He groaned. This would be hard. Half to two thirds of his class would not have magic, yet he had to try and find a lesson plan which kept even the magic users engaged. At the same time he could not estrange the muggles. He looked over the plan so far, shrugged, and got up to pour himself some more tea, staring into the swirling liquid inside the cup for a second as small parts of tea leaves floated down to the bottom.

He vaguely remembered reading somewhere that tea leaf reading had been big once upon a time. He was really reaching right now as he didn't even remember if he had read that in an actual book or in some magazine. Still, some had a gift for it, and the leading hypothesis was that it was a form of magic, albeit a low energy kind. People with little talent for magic could be very good at it. After a sip of tea he returned to the desk.

Class six: dig into other forms of magic like tea leaf reading, intuition and passive magic. Examine stories about mediums and discern fact from fiction. Permit students to share stories about that weird aunt 'who heard voices from heaven'.

That would bring him only half way through the semester, but for now it was enough preparation work. He could do a bigger test at that point so students would at least study. If he had learned one thing during his earlier years of teaching it was this fact: students will only study if they are tested on it, because that is what they are used to.

Furcifer sat back. It seemed like decades had passed since his last class, but in reality it had only been a few years. He had been more interested, more compassionate and caring. Now people annoyed him. Perhaps it was not people that really disturbed him, but just the fact that people were expected to do certain things. Excel in careers. Have healthy social lives. Make money and buy expensive things.

These things didn't interest him as much as most people. Sure, he appreciated not being out on the streets and having the university support his work, but when asked out by colleagues he would prefer to just stay in and study. There was so much to know and he could only do so little on his own... He just hoped that by the end of his run, other people would start researching magic.

He reviewed the lesson plan. It looked solid enough to him that he didn't feel bad putting it away for now.

The earlier notes on the bangle were moved aside to make more space for the red journal as Furcifer went digging for his findings on the magical simians he had encountered. It was very basic magic, but it had some similarities to magic used by earlier bloomers into magic. All in all it would prove an interesting first insight in magic. He noted down a few key points after reading through the first page of his findings.

Simians only use magic to fulfil needs. In mating season one or two will try and show off using magic, but these attempts are clumsy and often scare the female away at first. This has led to them being more secretive with magic in recent years and to use it only when it is necessary, for example to get a young one out of a precarious position or to obtain food from an unreachable area.

Furcifer sat back. It did show similarities with humans. There was no persecution of magic as such, magic was legal unless used for the purpose of a crime, but people were still hesitant to use it. He thought back about Manon, almost embarrassed to see him use magic in public because of how she was raised. Or Russell, who did not want to admit the effect of the magical bangle to him willingly? It seemed like they still had quite a way to go - but here he was preparing to teach a course on magic. Magic was seeping into the mainstream, and with that, the factions might come out as well. So far they were virtually unknown to anyone without magic, or would pose as normal, but exclusive institutions.

Life was strange. He got up and walked to the kitchen cabinet, pouring out his tea in order to pour himself some pinot noir. Perhaps it was time to wind down a bit right now. He took a whiff of the wine and settled back into his couch. By the time this glass was empty, he would probably have returned to the notes. But in this moment he did not feel bad about relaxing.

Chapter 6

Furcifer woke up, a page stuck to his cheek. With a grumble he pulled it loose, unaware of the writing it had left on his face, and rubbed his face. Great. He had fallen asleep researching again. This was how most of his evenings ended these days, with him sleeping on a pile of papers.

He stretched out and got up from the office chair, picking up the empty wine and tea stained mug. It was eight thirty in the morning, but he had a decent lesson plan for the first three lessons to show for his night of work.

Much of it had come back to him. How to shorten a class by skipping straight to exercises or making the exercise homework. How to lengthen it by dividing the class up in pairs, handing out exercises, and then pairing them up with others. How to deal with rowdy troublemakers by figuring out what they needed. It was surprising how little that knowledge had changed considering how much he had changed. In addition to these things he had learned how to order chai in

Hindi, how to make sure your stuff was not stolen on an overcrowded bus and how to stare down a youth who looked like he was about to rob you. He'd travelled more than he ever thought he would and it had been amazing. Before magic, he would have sat at home watching Strictly Come Dancing while grading papers. A more impressionable man might believe he was chosen for a destiny larger than himself. To change the world for the better with the time and powers meted out to him.

Luckily, even his ego wasn't that big. He walked over to the bathroom to wash his face so he could go get some breakfast from the cafeteria before they ran out of hashbrowns. He splashed some water into his face and took a deep breath, head filled with magic facts. It often happened that he could hardly think straight until he cleared his head properly and focussed on what needed to be done. This was how he would forgot to eat for a whole day or to drink water. His focus had led to amazing research, but it meant he needed to look out for himself. They would have a hard time finding a magic lecturer if he ended up in the hospital with malnutrition. Perhaps he should get a teaching assistant. Usually he looked for the most ambitious student during the first class and gave them the job. This approach rarely failed him in normal, mundane courses like philosophy. But in this case, the person he chose also had to be reliable and preferably understand the basics of just what magic was. Considering how few people even knew what magic was, that would be a hard task. He guessed he would

just have to keep an eye open during the first few
classes at least.

He dabbed his face dry on a towel and looked out of
the bathroom and over his living space.

The tower was even starting to feel like home now,
he realised. The smells of ink and tea were returning,
and a comfortable organised chaos was re-emerging
from the well organised drawers and cupboards. Even
things that had been stored in India were slowly
starting to come through and found a space in here -
questionable artefacts and letters which had been in
storage. It was interesting how few things he really
owned - a few things here and there, the rest were
books and gifts from other people. Especially the dean
had taken it upon herself to gift him a carpet and
some chairs and small furniture items to complement
the items already there. Personally, he didn't feel any
need for them and the chairs were now buried under
notebooks and loose papers anyway.

He would have to make an effort to organise today
- keep his own research, the research on the bangle
and course information and contents apart before they
merged into one pile of knowledge. He looked over the
pile, seeing a stray notebook page with a sketch of the
bangle on it.

The bangle... He had rarely thought of it again after
sending a hasty, inconclusive report to the museum
director saying that there was not yet enough
information available. The chemical tests he had
ordered hadn't come back yet, but that seemed to be
more because the university hadn't gotten around to

paying the bill just yet and he wasn't expecting to see any results the first three weeks. He wasn't going to chase it up - that was a useless endeavour. There was no way complaining here had ever made any change. The board moved slowly on any decision, from daily matters to grand galas, and he was only a lower level peon when it came to them.

Not like it mattered. The director had grabbed the report as a chance to call the artefact magical already, and the exhibition would be organised soon enough. They were just recruiting a new curator. Furcifer briefly wondered if the new curator would experience the same effects as Jeffrey had. If so, that would be interesting... He chuckled dryly and shaved his face. It had been a few days and he didn't want to look the way he did in Malaga again. A beard look hardly suited him, especially not in the bright red colour all of his hair now seemed to sprout in.

After the quick freshening up, he walked down the stairs towards the cafeteria. It was still early enough that there would be a queue, but they wouldn't be out of the most popular breakfast items. He crossed the long hall and ignored the strange looks he was getting. Perhaps he should change - he vaguely realised that this was the fifth day he was wearing this shirt. And a splash in the face was no substitute for a shower. He shrugged it off and walked over to the stack of trays.

Like every day it was the usual suspects. Students with hangovers, having a fatty breakfast in the hopes of dispelling the sickness. Their early professors enjoying their breakfast, and depending on their mood you could see whether it was before or after the class. And one or two pairs of parents stirring their coffee and waiting for their child to get out of class so they could visit their dorm. You could see them, talking softly among themselves, preparing mentally for whatever they would find there.

A TV played in the background, but the sound was too low for anyone to hear it. The subtitles were not very helpful either. However, when the museum appeared above a Breaking News bar, Furcifer was glued to the screen, inching along the queue and basically grabbing whatever he could without looking away from the report too much, stacking rolls onto fruit salads and grabbing the hash brown with his bare fingers, only barely noticing the heat. Shit, what was going on there? It didn't look like some airy announcement for the new exhibition.

Impatiently, he rushed out of the queue and flashed his badge at the disgruntled lunch lady. She mumbled something but he didn't care right now as the headlines became more specific. From the ominous "Break in at the Museum", the news anchor announced new developments and recapped the story. Furcifer rushed to a seat near the TV and turned the volume up magically.

"-We're just receiving more news about the break in at the museum. One curator has tragically lost his life in the break in, which seems to have happened around midnight last night. Apparently it is not uncommon for curators to work that late when preparing for a new exhibition. We were informed he and a security guard were the only people at the museum at that time. The director of the museum has announced that he will organise a press conference later today."

The anchor switched to a reporter on the scene, who did not have much more to add just yet. The exhibition had not been announced yet, so there was no way someone had already targeted it for such a political reason.

Unless it was someone who already knew – no. He could not go and assume the burglary and killing was because of the magical artefact. Perhaps it was an art heist. There were plenty of desirable items to steal there. As Furcifer dug into the breakfast he thought about this new development.

Crap. He would definitely have to contact the director just in case, but he really felt like something was off about this. Something happened this soon after his visit? He shook his head. It could hardly be a coincidence.

And if the item was missing, who knew what could happen to it.

This was all too convenient. A few days after he looked into this object, someone would try to steal it? Nobody could be that stupid. Unless...

Without even looking away from the TV, he put his messy breakfast tray onto the clearing belt. The looks from the now frankly furious cafeteria lady did not faze him in the least. He was already halfway out to the hallway.

Chapter 7

The museum stairs were slippery and many disappointed tourists stood nearby, hiding under umbrellas and looking onto city maps now that he museum was taken off of the to-do list. The grey sky seemed to have ruined many a day already. Some however, just seemed thrilled by the idea of a violent crime at the museum. Furcifer saw more than one pair of eager eyes every time the museum doors opened to let out an officer. Nobody, however, came close as the entrance was guarded by a police officer in uniform.

There was no way anyone who didn't need to be there was going to enter the museum today. Which meant Furcifer would have to sneak his way in. He was hoping to speak to director Donnovan himself and to figure out what had happened. If the bangle had gone missing, he wanted to know.

His break came when a tourist walked up to the agent to ask for directions, distracting him long enough for Furcifer to follow in a team of investigators in. He breezed past the initial receptionist who was busy speaking to the police before taking the elevator up to the director's office. He was glad he still remembered the way - the museum was a labyrinth if you were unfamiliar with its winding backstage areas.

The secretary's nook before Donnovan's office was empty. With a frown he knocked and entered, seeing the director startle. The man instantly got up and buttoned his jacket.

"Oh, it's you." The director sighed. "You must be the first non-uniformed person I've seen today." Furcifer could hear the relief in his voice. Donnovan nodded to a chair where he could sit down and Furcifer obeyed, if only because he needed the man to trust and confide in him right now. As he sat down, Donnovan sat down again as well.

"So, your secretary's not in today?" He started neutrally.

"Poor boy discovered the body when he came in this morning. He's had to talk to the police all day, I don't envy him." He sighed and took off his glasses to clean them. "So did you just come to see some mayhem?"

"Actually... I was wondering if all this had to do with the bangle."

The director shot up straight in his seat and stared at him for a second, before speaking again.

"Yes. Yes it does." He sighed.

"The bangle seems to have been what they came in for. Marty, the new curator, was cleaning it and preparing it for a visit of the insurance expert who was supposed to come by today. We had hoped to get it evaluated today, before we start this whole thing, you know, costs..." He shrugged and looked to the man.

"Was it stolen?" The director was giving him too much information and he only needed to know one thing.

"We don't know. The box it was in is nowhere to be found. It is alarmed, so that when it is opened without the proper key, it will send out an alert to us. No alarm has been triggered so far."

"So for all you know it's still in the museum." This was bad. A possible magical item on the loose in this chaos, where one could easily steal it... He shot up.

"Let me go and help look for it." He offered. Perhaps his intuition would help with this. He had felt how the bangle sensed.

Donnovan stifled a laugh. "Don't be ridiculous, Mr. Furcifer. I cannot have you rooting around the museum looking for a single item in this chaos!" The man said. "When we find it you will be informed."

"One, the item is magical." He had not wanted to drop that bomb until he was absolutely certain, but it looked like they didn't leave him much choice. The curator's eyes widened slightly, but he only gave a small, grave nod. Obviously he had anticipated that result.

"Secondly it clearly has an effect on whoever touches it." Furcifer tried not to let the lack of reaction deflate him

"Jeffrey, your last curator, passed a psych test just a month before the incident. In fact, I bet you did not press charges because you believe the boy's career has a decent chance of recovering from this!"

It would have been perfect publicity for the museum. A blown up scandal, slightly exaggerated to make the curator sound even worse than he was. Publicity from the papers, blogs, anything who would be interested. It would make the exhibition infamous before it even had a start date. However, the usually press hungry director had played it safe. That had been his first clue that the director had second thoughts about all this.

Donnovan momentarily looked defeated and sighed. "Yes. I did... believe the boy is sane. Whatever happened... there was no damage done." He said, looking up as if to explain himself.

Furcifer shrugged. "I don't care how or what. I just need you to realise the gravity of the situation." This could be bad. If the item was not located... He took a deep breath.

"You know what? You're going to use my help whether you want it or not." He got up and started towards the door.

Donnovan sighed as he got up.

"I hate to do this to you, kid... But... Officers! Get this man out of here!"

The same rubberneckers who had been eagerly watching the door once again perked up as a red headed man was shoved out the door without much decorum. Furcifer hissed but merely straightened his hoodie and flipped up his hood.

That had gone worse than planned. At least he had spoken his mind to the director, and whatever happened next was on his head.

Kid! He had called him a kid! How dared he. He glared up at the director's window and walked away.

Chapter 8

Furcifer banged at the door, hearing a groan come from inside the room. At least he was in. The door opened, and he could see a paused Netflix show on the television. Jeffrey himself was still dressed in his pajamas despite it being one in the afternoon now.

"You again!" He visibly stifled a yawn.

"Yes, me." Furcifer made his way into the house. "The bangle. Do you still have the connection with it?"

"What? If I'm near, I may feel it, but – "

"We need to locate it." Furcifer spread out a map of the area.

"Wait, what? Are you saying…"

"I'm saying, yes, it may have been stolen. The museum doesn't know where it is but I'm guessing you understand better than the director why we should find this thing and keep it locked up." He looked over. "Right?" He asked.

"Yeah..." Jeffrey nodded weakly. "Look... I don't see how a map is going to help."

The map was extensive, covering most of the city in great detail. He took a deep breath. That was a lot of ground to cover to find one missing bangle that could easily hide on a woman's wrist.

"Close your eyes. Focus. Focus all your energy, all your thoughts. Focus solely on that piece of metal. How it felt to you. What you smelled when you touched it. Everything." Furcifer positioned Jeffrey in front of the map. "Forget everything else. There is only the bangle right now."

Furcifer lowered his voice to an almost droning sound. Slowly, he could see that the man was concentrating. He took a step back when the man put a hand out over the map. The man's face relaxed as he let his hand drift over the map, from the university, to the library, the main plaza... before finally resting on top of an area about a mile north of the museum.

"There."

"Ugh..." Furcifer groaned. "An area full of pawnshops and drug dealers." He zipped up his hoodie.

"Might as well look the part." He shrugged.

Jeffrey groaned. "Do I have to go?"

"Yes. You're the one who can feel its presence." He looked around and raised an eyebrow at Russell, who was sipping some coffee and who looked away as Furcifer glanced over to him.

"Hey, want to come shopping with us?"

Chapter 9

"This was like... The worst idea ever." Sighed Jeffrey as they walked into the area, his breath forming a small cloud of vapour. He had insisted his car be parked a few blocks away so they wouldn't risk it being stolen or burned down. The area itself was residential, but with a lot of closed shops, little alleyways, dollar stores and pawn stores. One cheery manicure place tried to liven up the place, but it just looked sad amidst the grey buildings. It made for a sombre walk.

"No, it's not." Furcifer held out a bead on a string of wool and loosely tied it around their wrists. "If you get into trouble, break this. It will teleport you to a friend of mine." He said.

"Only if you're in trouble. Magic sightings make an area kind of jumpy." Still, these kinds of areas where all the same. People peering out of windows only to never have seen anything when the police asked. They would be pretty safe.

"Now come on." He motioned the two to get moving towards the first pawnshop, pausing in front of it calmly. Still, this didn't make sense. Lots of valuables in the museum to pawn off, why a bracelet? Perhaps the thief had just picked something inconspicuous. The bracelet is strange combination of being discreet and attractive might have lured the thief into stealing it.

"Feeling anything?"

"No." Sighed Jeffrey.

"This is stupid. He's not some magic smelling dog!" Argued Russell, though he was quick to follow Furcifer when the mage walked away.

"Wait." A few shops down, Jeffrey hesitated. "This is the one."

"You sure?"

A nod. "It's here." The skin on his hands had clear goose bumps.

"Alright. Stay here." He grabbed Russell and started to go in.

"Why me." Whispered Russell.

"Because Jeffrey acts weird around the bangle." He looked around the shop. The usual fare, if a little more antique looking than most shops. In the array of copper lamps and statues, the bangle would be nearly invisible.

"Scuse me!" Furcifer adopted his best New York accent. "My friend here is looking for something special for the wifey. You know, we've both been out a bit too late and maybe a little gift will ease the pain, you know what I'm saying? She's classy though, really into rings and bracelets. And like gold. But not real gold, or we wouldn't be shopping here would we Jack?" He amicably patted his friend on the shoulder.

Russell faked his best smile and reverted to his farm accent.

"That's right. Classy girl. Any nice bracelets or some shit?" He looked around the display case nonchalantly, and Furcifer had to admit he was doing pretty well.

The shopkeeper shrugged. If he had noticed their act was merely theatrical, he didn't show it, or more likely, didn't care. If he sold something he would be happy.

The old man took out a box and dumped it onto the counter. Silver, gold plated, copper and other bracelets formed a small pile. He looked up, shrugged and stepped back enough to let them choose. Nothing stood out. The place was rundown, with no sign of anything else going on. No sounds in a suspicious backroom or people hustling around nervously – just a man and his shop.

Furcifer hesitated. This didn't make sense. He could feel the bracelet presence but it was not here. One of the items had been hexed to have the same magic signature, leading them here. That made more sense. Why would anyone kill a curator just to sell the bracelet in a rundown pawn shop? Art was usually stolen to order, not because it was shiny. Russell seemed to pick up on the hesitation, especially as he didn't see a single bracelet looking like the one described to him. He grabbed a silver one with a one dollar tag – it looked more like a large hoop earring than a bracelet – and quickly paid the price for it.

"I think she'll like that one!" Russell grinned convincingly.

"Let's go. Thanks for saving my butt! I was going to buy flowers at this time of night..."

Furcifer chuckled relieved. The old shopkeeper was scooping all the bracelets up into their box again and didn't even watch as they left. A good sign. As they approached the door, however, Furcifer heard the click of a breaking bead.

"Shit!" He hissed and rushed out the store.

There was just a puff of smoke where Jeffrey had been waiting. Around the smoke, however, three thugs were gathered. Dark jackets, worn jeans, steel toed boots and faces which had obviously kissed the pavement more than once. One with patchy green hair seemed to be the leader, quite upset that the man had vanished.

"Where'd he go! Bob!" He hissed at a taller man, built like a tank. He didn't look very smart, however, and looked around him.

"Yeah, time to go!" Furcifer said, looking to Russell. "Bead!"

Russell backed away and hastily slid the bracelet off of his wrist, loudly slamming it against the wall he was retreating towards. As it broke, a quick flash of smoke enveloped him and–

Next thing he knew he was lying on his back on a cushy blue rug. From the floor he could see some furniture, a few book cases and a pair of legs walking towards him.

Aiden crouched down by the man.

"Hey. It's okay. You're safe. Can you sit up? Furcifer warned me this would be your first bead." He helped Russell sit up before holding a hand up and summoning a glass of water towards it.

"Have a sip. It helps."

Russell looked around the cosy lounge. On another couch, Jeffrey was already curled up, shoes kicked off hastily so he could have his feet on the seat. A blanket was drawn around him and he was sipping a cup of water as well.

"How long has he-" Russell cleared his hoarse throat, before sipping the water handed to him. It did help - the familiar feeling grounded him. The change had been so sudden his body had been unsure how to deal with it.

"Just a few minutes." Aiden said. The man looked young, maybe thirty, with shoulder length black hair and green eyes.

"He arrived here just a bit ago, also by bead. You must have missed him by just a few seconds."

Furcifer appeared as well, but with more decorum - he landed on his feet and immediately straightened up.

"Thanks, Ai." He said.

Aiden shrugged. "My pleasure." He turned back to Russell. "I'm Aiden Willemeens."

"Russell Marson." Russell sipped the water, finding it did help his throat.

"Did you find what you were looking for?" Aiden went to sit in another couch, picking up a cup of tea from the lounge table in between the couches.

"No. I am starting to think it was a setup - whoever it was knew Jeffrey would be there and I stupidly left him out on his own."

"It could have just been robbers..." Jeffrey said meekly. "I mean... I did look out of place." He still sounded nervous.

"The bangle wasn't there. Maybe it was, but it was not in the store. I think someone hexed another item to seem similar and planted it there." Furcifer ran a hand through his hair.

"If they were after Jeffrey, it might be that they need more information about the item." Russell theorised.

"That's what I was thinking." Furcifer looked over. "We will have to proceed very carefully with this. Someone is trying to pull our strings."

"About strings. What was in that bead?" Asked Jeffrey.

Aiden chuckled. "My own invention. A pre-programmed spell poured into liquid glass." He said. "I make them on demand." He shrugged and sat back.

"I forgot to mention. This is Aiden's house. He's got the only magic store in the city." Furcifer explained. "Most mage-y people get their supplies from here or the internet."

Aiden looked over. "I'm pretty sure they're not interested, Furcifer." He said. "Suffice to say you're safe here. The house is warded with all kinds of good things."

Perhaps it was rude, but Aiden had a tendency to simplify all talk of magic when he wasn't sure about a person's abilities. The one seemed like he might have some talent, the other just... Seemed to wonder whether he had fallen down a rabbit hole and into a new world.

Russell sighed. "So what now?"

"So you go home." Said Furcifer. "I dragged you into this needlessly. You should go home. If they're after Jeffrey..." He shook his head. There was no way he could guarantee his safety until he had figured out what was going on.

Aiden looked up. "He can stay here. Help out in the store." He shrugged.

Furcifer nodded thoughtfully. This would be the last place they would come looking for him. It was hard, if not impossible, to follow a bead teleportation with magical means. Without magic there was no way to trace it.

"No!" Jeffrey looked up. "No. It was probably just some muggers, and I panicked. So I got the location of the bangle wrong. It was a stupid plan of yours and –" He sighed. "I'd like to go home now."

Russell nodded. "He's probably right, Furcifer. If they got into the museum they would be able to access his records. You think that if they could circumvent the alarm, they would be deterred by a locked file cabinet? There is no way they would set up this elaborate trap you're imagining." He agreed.

Furcifer sighed deeply. "Fine. Go home." He rubbed the bridge of his nose.

Aiden got up and grabbed some more beads. "Use these if you ever want to come back here. There's a taxi rank just outside the mall, around the corner." He handed them a small collection of beads and saw them out, before turning back to Furcifer. The man was sitting back in the couch, eyes closed as he thought about the night. After a few minutes he opened his eyes again.

Furcifer looked around to the pictures on the wall. Pictures of Aiden in grand magical acts, with pretty assistants holding card decks and standing on grand stages under banners reading "Aiden the Astonishing" in large letters. They looked out of place in the almost old fashioned lounge and contrasted sharply with the current image of Aiden, looking tired and wearing a holey cardigan over an old t-shirt and pajama pants.

"Do you miss it?" The redhead asked.

"Sometimes." He had to admit. "It was nice. Travelling. Lots of money, gorgeous women." He looked over one of the photos with the assistants. Sometimes he did feel nostalgic.

"Why'd you quit then?" He asked, looking over to him.

"Well... Mostly because, this magic thing came so quickly. I just woke up and boom." He snapped his fingers. "What if it vanishes again?"

"Oooh..." He nodded. "People would realise you're a fraud." He grinned widely.

Aiden laughed. "Kind of." He said, looking over. "Jeeze. You still don't mince your words."

Furcifer chuckled. "Never will, never did. Still glad to see you come back from Vegas and settling down."

"Yeah. Settling down." There were still boxes he hadn't unpacked, mostly ones to do with his acts. He took a deep breath and got up.

"You should head home. I need to open the shop early tomorrow for a customer picking up a package." He started picking up the glasses and looked to Furcifer.

"And stay safe, you idiot."

Furcifer did feel like he had gone off the rails. How could he have been so wrong about the bangle's location? Getting involved in criminal investigations had not been in the job description. What was he even doing chasing this thing?

Maybe they were right. Jeffrey had not shown any inclination towards magical talent ever, and suddenly scryed the item very precisely. Perhaps it had just been suggestion by Furcifer, more than anything. The gang outside? Jeffrey had looked pretty out of place. New to the area and nervously hanging around outside a pawn shop alone. Easy target.

He scoffed at himself. He couldn't let it get to him! He had been wrong before. A long, long time ago.

Furcifer shook his head. "Jeffrey, you go home. Give me your car keys and I'll bring it back to you."

"You have a driver's license?" Jeffrey questioned.

Furcifer shrugged. "It's only slightly out of date..."

A groan. "I'm not going back there either way." He tossed the keys over.

Furcifer teleported back to where they had come from. It would not do to leave Jeffrey's car out in a bad neighbourhood like this - there was a good chance it would no longer be there when they came back after all. Last thing he wanted was for the man to become uncooperative because of the bad experience and the fact his car had been stolen. He was sure that would come back on him. After all he'd dragged Jeffrey and Russell into this mess without a care for how they might feel about any of it. Jeffrey had a thing for sensing where the bracelet could be, and Russell... Well, he was just more relaxed than Jeffrey. Jeffrey was much too tense, too worried. Taking Russell into the shop had aroused a lot less suspicion.

Cute little country boy in a big city, he thought with a chuckle. *He was strangely charming and probably knew how to use that to his advantage. He and Aiden seemed to get on very well, at least. Though he probably got on very well with everyone.*

He sighed and sauntered over to the shop they had visited earlier, trying to retrace their steps. They'd parked about a block away, but to the left or the right?

Finally, he decided to try left first. Deep in thought he crossed the street.

The first thing he heard was the engine of a car revving, before it hit him squarely in the side. He hissed and fell over, trying to sit up to figure out what had just happened. He'd been hit by an accelerating car? What idiot would accelerate near a pedestrian crossing? His thoughts became disjointed as his vision lost focus.

"Does he have it?" A female voice. Someone crouched down by him and started searching his pockets.

"No!" The man replied after a thorough search, including his wrists. That was funny – what were they looking for?

"Then call an ambulance. We have to go." The woman again. He barely heard the car door close before he passed out.

Just a few blocks away, a gang filed out of the alleyway. A green haired man hit a tall bruiser over the head until he gave up the stolen purse.

"Bloody hell Bob. That's almost two robberies you screwed over." He sighed, grabbing the purse and rifling through it. "Oooh! Xanax!" He grinned and confiscated the pill bottle, walking by the unconscious mage.

When he woke up, he felt the sun on his face. Squinting, he looked around. A bland room – much like a hospital.

"Where am I?" He tried to sit up, but a nurse held him back.

"Zeus city hospital. You were hit by a car. How are you feeling?" He did some quick checks.

"I'm fine. When can I go?"

"We'll let you know. It will probably be today if someone can come pick you up."

Furcifer sighed. The dean was his emergency contact, so she would find out first. This was not going to be fun.

"So uh, you'll back me up when my boss doesn't believe I was hit by a car, right?" He tried to joke at the nurse.

Chapter 10

Furcifer spent the next few days between his tower apartment and the cafeteria. There were mostly bruises to be healed up, which he could combine easily with his work. He was preparing for his classes and found himself getting quite into it, honestly. It was nice. It was a change of pace from the bangle, which seemed to have vanished without a trace. The museum was slowly opened up again, though the office where the curator had been found dead was still closed.

Jeffrey had been weirdly quiet. He hadn't heard from the man ever since the search for the item nor had he tried to contact him. He didn't care much - they weren't friendly as such in Furcifer's eyes. In fact he would even consider Manon more of a friend.

And today was the first day of his class. With a sigh he rifled through his wardrobe trying to find something somewhat fitting. He finally found a pair of new-ish pants, a clean shirt and a jacket that looked decent. A far cry from his nice suits and casual smart outfits which he used to wear when he taught a class.

As a last touch, he combed his hair then tied it back into a low ponytail. A peek in the mirror told him it would do for the day. Perhaps he would get back into dressing nicely, but he doubted it. To dress nice cost time - both to go shopping and to put together outfits that worked. If he got to a haircut within a few months, it would be a big victory.

He saw Manon look up when he entered, grinning widely. She had, of course, taken a seat in the front row and was now holding up a little sign that said "Go professor!"

"You take that down." He said, looking at her sternly.

"Aww... I worked all morning on that."

"I would have hoped you would have worked on actually preparing for class." He raised an eyebrow and looked around the half-filled auditorium.

"You didn't say anything about preparing for class." Another voice piped up. A young man, with shaggy blonde hair.

"I lied." Furcifer said. "Get used to it." He walked over to the desk, confiscating the sign on his way there.

Furcifer set his shoulder bag down on the desk and glared around.

He turned around with a huff and started writing on the table.

"My name is Atze Furcifer. I spent the last two years travelling and studying magic. Before all that I studied philosophy. I graduated with a few degrees in history and philosophy and taught both these courses here at this university. When magic appeared I found I had some." Understatement, but he didn't want to start the course bragging too much.

"I started studying it by just trying things and noting down findings. The university showed interest in those findings and I started to do research." He looked around.

"Well then. Enough about me." He picked up a box of books. "Don't tell anyone. I had these printed at the copy shop with my print card." The "textbooks" were barely more than ringed copies with a plastic cover and back, but they were cheap to make and he only needed around thirty, so there was no need to look for anything larger scaled. He picked up a small stack and passed one down every row.

"Awesome! Free books!" Manon grinned, grabbing one and passing the rest of the stack on.

Twitch chuckled and took the stack from Manon. "Thanks." He said and passed the rest on. This would prove interesting! He hadn't expected much from this course but it would at least be entertaining,

Furcifer found it easy to fall back into his routine. It came almost naturally to feel the mood of the class, to adjust the pace or speed it up, or to let the class take charge for a while by leading them into a discussion.

All he had to do to unleash that discussion was present the case of the apes with magic, then let them run with it. It was almost fun to hear their new, but often silly ideas when it came to the magic mammals.

"Alright, class is over. I need you to read up on all you can find about the history of magic... But you can only use materials without my name on it." He knew those were hard to find. From the groan coming from the classroom they knew as well. At least they had come prepared. That would make it a lot more fun - a motivated class was simple to teach. And the hardest work was done. Interest was sparked, whether that had been before class or during, but he had not seen anyone yet who could fill the position of teaching assistant. Except for one, perhaps.

As he put away the remaining books, Manon rushed over and tapped him on the shoulder.

"That was amazing!" She smiled. "Must be cool - to travel like that then get to teach it to interested youths."

"Interested, you call it?" He chuckled. "You were barely staying awake."

"That had more to do with the early hour you choose to teach your class." She waved a hand dismissively.

"Yes. Two post meridian. So early. Please forgive me." Snorted Furcifer. "Make yourself useful and pick up that stack of books. I'll grab the elevator up to the tower, so if you can just help me get them there I will give you the questions to the pop quiz for next week."

"You serious?" Her eyes went wide at that proposition.

"I'm still looking for a teaching assistant." Furcifer said.

"Too much responsibility. I wouldn't take it seriously enough." Shrugged Manon, walking with Furcifer to the elevator. "Jessica seems like an intelligent girl though. Maybe her?"

"Smart of you to be aware." Furcifer complimented, a rare occurrence for him. He seldom found himself impressed by non-mages. He had seen so many and so much, and he realised that his standards were sometimes too high. Which didn't mean he would ease up in any way.

Furcifer pushed the button for the elevator and looked over Manon. Even in torn jeans and with a messy ponytail, a far cry from the summer dress and uniform cardigan, the girl looked confident and authoritative. She actually paid attention in class. Even more so, she had even raised some valid points during the group debate. Perhaps it was not a good thing she considered herself too irresponsible to take the job - it would only lead to her underperforming and staying within her comfort zone.

"Manon?"

"Yeah?" The girl shifted the box of books a little higher up in her grip.

"You just got the teaching assistant job. Congratulations." He just hoped he wasn't making a mistake giving her the position of teaching assistant.

Chapter 11

Perhaps he had made a mistake giving Manon the position of teaching assistant.

Not that she was doing a bad job – quite the opposite. It had been two weeks since she had been appointed and she was doing amazingly. She prepped the classroom before every class, graded simple pop quizzes and was the first point of call for students with questions about the course.

The mistake was in making it easy on himself. Furcifer found himself rolling up to class five minutes late and nearly unprepared, going off of his prepared course structure without much extra meat on it and going for more and more group discussions or veering off into what he had just been studying in order to keep himself interested. The case of the bangle had come to a standstill, but he was still intrigued by it. Despite the progress, he was still working through it, trying to find any leads.

Today was the rare day he had actually given a bit more than just the bare minimum. There had been quite a bit of theory to chow through and he had skipped last class's load, so he had powered through what was perhaps the largest... chapter in his course book, the history of magic. It had been quite a lot – he had gathered a lot of information on the subject and had even written a dissertation about this. It had been received very well, with many peers considering it the first and best of its kind. Not that there had been much to compare it to just yet, which frustrated Furcifer to no end. His field was nearly empty and he was only just getting started, yet he was considered to be the top of his field.

He guessed that's why this class was so important. To get more people interested. To get people to care for the magic in this world.

"And so far we've only seen a few million users of magic come forward. So any questions?" Furcifer finished his long lecture. A dozen hands shot up and Furcifer raised an eyebrow.

"No? That's great. You can take it from here, Manon." He announced before leaving the classroom.

Manon sighed exasperatedly and got up to take the questions. She had become quite used to this kind of behaviour by now. But working together with Furcifer had also brought some perks.

She was learning spells much faster than anyone else, just because Furcifer would let her into his tower and let her browse his note books. Sometimes she would spend entire evenings just reading all the things Furcifer had observed, described, ruled out and confirmed.

Manon looked around the classroom. "Yes, you." She nodded to one of the guys in the back who had his hand up high.

"Could uh, you repeat all that?" The overwhelmed student asked timidly.

Chapter 12

*W*orkings of magic.

While magic hasn't been perceived to be around for very long, it's a simple force. It is easiest to compare to electricity. It can be generated but not destroyed and in the right way can be used for pretty much anything.

One way to generate magic, is spells. Spells are like sentences in that they should have a grammatical structure containing direction, effect and duration. 'I need my magic to go that way, do this and I want the effect to stay for this long.' More complicated spells can include more factors, like amount of people affected, when the effect happens or just who it targets.

Spells work in any language, but the user's native language is preferred as it will cause the fewest misunderstandings when wielding such powers. Still, spells in Esperanto have been common due to the simple grammar of the language and the ease of translating them into other languages without misunderstandings. While the language for a spell can be as flowery as one prefers, shorter spells seem to have the least chance of backfiring.

Also, one needs to focus for the entire duration of the spell's pronunciation, in which case "lumon" was a lot easier and shorter to shout than "chase away the darkness and free the light" for a lighting spell.

Much like all devices use energy differently, all spells use magic differently. There are some basic techniques which magic users can use to direct their magical power.

The easiest is to use a conductor – an item like a wand or a broom. These help to aim the spell, thus meaning the user can focus on the spell and does not need to insert directional phrases into the magic. This shortens spells, sometimes to even a few words. There, do this. An extra advantage is that some materials, a few kinds of rare woods, can multiply the effect of the magic.

Magic can still be used without wands or conductors, but this is considered an advanced technique. Even without words, hand gestures need to be used to direct the magic even if the user has no specific direction in mind.

As far as we know, few things can not be done with magic. One can not change another's emotional state with magic. One can not use magic to kill directly. One can not permanently make things disappear. Even if you make something vanish, it will show up after a while again. Even if you cannot tell where or when. It will reappear.

Between his academic writings and the forbidden spell books, Furcifer had written down about three fourths of what was currently known about magic. Mind, this did not mean that he actually had discovered all this – just that he had been the first to write it down and make it available. This did mean that there wasn't much of a magic community yet. It was to be expected when the centre of the scene was a grumpy old man who preferred to lock himself up in his tower over speaking to others.

Furcifer could hear Manon basically rehash the class for the students as he walked away. He felt a little bad for the kid, but then he realised that if it wasn't for her he would have to do all that. And that made him happy he had taken her on as his assistant. She put up with his shit.

"Excuse me." Twitch had rushed after the lecturer. "I think you're wrong about the appearance of magic global." He said, trying to keep up with the man.

Furcifer groaned. "I have no consultation hour today, and I definitely won't open the floor to class discussion for such foolishness next class." He pushed the button for the elevator and looked over to the small man. "That debate is purely academic."

"It doesn't just appear everywhere at once. It appears in waves." Twitch said,

Furcifer looked over to the man. "Look..."

He frowned as he tried to remember the student's name.

"Twitch. I mean. Asa. People just call me Twitch."

"Asa..."

"No Twitch is fine! I didn't mean anything...."

"Twitch. There is no way anyone could prove magic did not just appear globally at one point. The affected percentage is small enough that it just looks like patterns."

"It's not patterns. It's a wave."

"Humans love to see patterns."

"I know what I'm talking about. Certain DNA groups, affected at a certain time, getting magic. There are correlations!"

The elevator doors slid shut as Furcifer closed his eyes. Too late to push the man out.

"There is not enough research yet to prove any of that! As said. This is a completely academic debate." Furcifer looked over.

"But what if it wasn't? What if I could show you a spell book from the middle ages describing such a wave of magic? I have notes and findings and books..." The man's stubbornness was making him less careful than he should be.

Furcifer's head jerked over, much to Twitch's satisfaction.

"There is no way you could have that." He said.

"But what if I did? Oh, this looks like my floor." He adjusted his shoulder bag and got out on the third floor – which was nowhere near where he needed to be as his dorm room wasn't even in this building. Still, it would be faster to get back from here than from the top floor.

"Hold on." Furcifer sighed. "I would... love to see these... findings you have."

"It would be my pleasure." He still got out of the elevator, having gotten what he wanted.

"It was nice to meet you. My name is Asa Ward" Twitch nodded. "How about I come by during your consultation hour?"

Furcifer groaned. "You know I don't have those, right?"

"I do." Smiled Twitch. "But you might want to make time for this." Okay, grabbing the attention of one of the foremost researchers and scholars of magic had made him a little proud. As long as he stayed careful, though, he should be okay. He got out of the elevator and waved a second before walking off. Only when the doors had closed did he start looking around for the stairs, embarrassed he had pretty much gotten lost on his own campus.

...

Asa Ward. Furcifer pondered over the name He'd seen it before. A. Ward. The author of the oldest account on magic. Before he could even react the doors of the elevator to stop the man getting away they had slid shut already.

Chapter 13

"Keep focussing. He raised an eyebrow at the students looking up from their papers. He'd put a lot of effort into the test for today. It wasn't as if he could just let Manon write up the test - she would know the answers! He had asked her to write a list of a hundred questions, then had selected ten of the most difficult looking ones for the test. Manon gave him more glares than the rest of the students for that move, but he did not care. He just shrugged at her and sat back in his seat.

He thought back about the bangle. The trace had gone cold. The museum board was not sure what to do next, but they were talking to the university about hiring Furcifer to track the item down once the semester ended. It wasn't as if he had prepared for the rest of the year already anyway.

He looked over one of the paper handouts left on the table and looked over the questions on the sheet. They all had to do with long-lasting magic and residual magic. He had found himself at such a standstill that maybe it was not such a bad idea to let his students' brains loose on the questions he was asking himself. What was the use of putting a spell that drove people delusional on an item made for daily wear? Was it some sort of convoluted attempt at making someone doubt their own judgement? A nasty prank played on someone decades ago?

Manon rushed over and handed her paper over, with a little played salute before taking her seat again.

Furcifer sighed and looked over the page she had just handed in. Sure enough, every question had been filled in. What else could he have expected from her? His eyes scanned the answers.

Q2: A long term magic spell is a low level magic spell which has an effect for an indefinite amount of time. Which uses would such a spell have?

A: As a map or marker. Spell can be used to identify who has access and attract the ones who are authorized. For example, such a spell could theoretically have been placed on Excalibur to make sure only Arthur found it.

Furcifer paused. Of course. The bangle wanted to be found by the person who could wield it and who would be able to figure out what it wanted. If it recognised Jeffrey was not that person, it could cause him harm and make him take it off. Instead he had continued to pine after it even though they had been separated. For some reason, the bangle had latched onto him. So why had he been unable to locate it? He should have been drawn to it like a magnet. Unless he was lying.

He sat up, beginning to understand why the culprits of the museum murders had not been found, or the bangle. Jeffrey had planned all of this. Perhaps even their failed little adventure to the pawn shop to make sure they lost the trail.

"Oi. Manon. You up for an adventure?"

The woman looked up from her desk. "Depends on what you mean by that." She said, her auburn ponytail bouncing as her head shot up.

Chapter 14

Furcifer had dragged the student up to his room to look over the documents as soon as he could. A few hours had passed since the test and the heat of the day was starting to dissipate. His tower was nice and cool, partly because of a cooling spell.

"I've seen this magic before in the Canutta library. It's fallen into disuse due to the side effects...." Said Manon.

"No shit. So someone in your faction could have easily done this?"

"Yes, but what are you implying?" She frowned, looking over to him.

"Not implying. Just stating. Your faction has been against magic being made public – why not target a curator working on a possible magic exhibition?"

"Chicken and egg much? This spell was put on it before it was found and we would not bait anyone on the off chance... ugh. You've clearly never been part of a faction."

"I count myself lucky there." He shrugged. "You get biased. Bias leads to bad research."

"Yet the scribes alone have more information than you'll ever learn on your own." She raised an eyebrow before returning to the page she was reading. Furcifer decided to let that one slide, but she was right. He would give his right arm to spend a week in the Scribe archives.

It does look like a marker..." She decided, looking over the notes again. "It would make the wearer feel possessive so she – or he – wouldn't forget to wear it. But as long as it is worn it would lead the owner to where they need to be." She looked back over to the papers "This doesn't look very legit." She made a face at Furcifer, hoping to change the subject away from her faction. Furcifer knew his stance on factions made her uneasy. She had always lived inside a faction and could not imagine being alone with her magic.

"Totally is. I made the copies myself." Furcifer smiled, hoping to defuse the tension.

"So we need to figure out where they're going next..." He tapped his chin. If the new theory was correct, the effect of the bangle has lead Jeffrey to murder the curator while pleading ignorance and setting them on the wrong trail when they tried to find the bangle. Right now be could not assume the man was innocent. He had to figure out if the man was wilfully deceiving them, and why.

He had been one step ahead all this time already and Furcifer had not realised. Worse, he had told him about his methods and his own magic. It would give the man an advantage if he went into hiding. There was also a large chance a third party was involved –

the party who had hit him with their car had checked his wrists - and unless they were really complex and compassionate heisters who called ambulances for their victims, the chance that this had to do with the bracelet was a lot bigger.

Which is why he had decided to involve Manon. Her answer had given him the breakthrough he had needed. She thought differently from him and could be a valuable ally.

"So what kind of thing would a map on a bangle lead to?"

"If it's designed to look like women's jewellery, it might be a woman's prized possessions. But still. Why a bangle? A pair of earrings would be more secure as you'd need both items..." She took a deep breath and let it out again. "A necklace, however, is easy to steal or break."

Furcifer nodded.

"It's very plain. Could easily have been designed for a man." He added.

She could be onto something there... He had never considered the item itself much, too focussed on the magic and whether or not it had any. A low level magic spell like they were thinking about now could be very hard to detect if the person it was meant for was not nearby. So if he found the bracelet on Jeffrey... It would be a lot easier to figure out what it did.

Furcifer sighed. He was sure that he had been played now. He looked around to Manon.

"You go and get some rest." He said. He did not want to involve his students more than he had to. Twitch maybe. That one at least looked old enough to be responsible. And he had a spellbook which could be useful. If the magic was as old as the bracelet, the mage's book might have a clue of where it had come from.

He got up and ushered the student out before locking the door behind her.

Finding Twitch's home hadn't been hard. The man lived on the campus, so his address was registered in his file. Furcifer rapped at the door impatiently and then stood back, waiting for the man to open. Crap. He just hoped this would work out. A lot of his plan depended on the fact that the man would actually let him see the spellbook he was talking about.

Twitch opened up, dressed in lounge pants and a t shirt. It had been a few hours since class and he obviously had not expected company.

"Uh... Hi."

He blinked, clearly surprised to see Furcifer at the door. "Hi." Furcifer looked over and walked in. "You told me about this spell book you had?"

"Yes." He nodded, walking to his room to find the spellbook he had. A few minutes later he came out with a beautiful, leather bound tome with depressed designs on it. It was a beautiful old book - lovingly repaired quite often. Furcifer remembered what the man had told him about it. He had repaired the cover and now he was working on digitising the spells, by scanning the pages and also typing in any text on the pages into a word document so that the two could be combined into one file. A wealth of knowledge for his own faction, the scribes. A shame, really. Nobody outside of the faction would ever be able to read the spells in this book.

Furcifer rather roughly took the book from Twitch and started reading through it. "Here it is!" He huffed and found the page he was looking for. "This must be like the spell that was used on the bangle..." He read through a lingering spell, apparently used to bring dear things together again – whether family or possessions.

"The bangle?" Frowned Twitch. "You're not making sense, sir."

"Furcifer. My name is Furcifer." He looked over to him. "Thanks though. I do like a good Sir-ing from time to time. Makes me feel respected." He took a deep breath.

"An artefact was stolen from the museum, and it had a low level magic to it. I suspect it is actually a sort of... finding spell." He showed the page he had been reading.

"Look. I think this was the point of the spell. To link to something or.... someone hidden. It is entirely possible the spell lasted a few centuries, according to this book. So if they were hiding a person, that person would be dead and the magic undone. If it leads to an item the item should provide a clue." He tapped his lips and sighed. "And I want to know where this trail goes." He grinned a little and found himself getting lost in thought as he considered all the new information.

It was quiet for a few minutes until Twitch sighed.

"So why do you need to know where this spell leads to?" He finally asked.

"Well!" Furcifer sat up. "I don't need to know. I'm just curious. Especially as someone already died for this."

"What?" Twitch went wide eyed. "You need to go to the police with this!"

"With what? Oh, I think a man I know killed a curator to steal a bangle. Expensive? Oh no, just a copper bracelet. Why did he do it? Just to try and find something. We don't know what though." Twitch raised an eyebrow. "They'd love that. Think before you speak, Snitch."

"Twitch." Twitch sighed and looked over, his left eye's twitch playing up at the man's sudden intrusion and mockery. "So what are you going to do then? Let him get away with it?"

"No. I'm going to steal it and see if I can make it show me what it does. He doesn't know I know yet." He smirked a little and looked over.

"Uhuuuh... And what if he does?" He raised an eyebrow.

"Well..." Furcifer sighed. The man had been a few steps ahead every bit of the way so far. What if he did know? He sighed. He had been eluded before. He had been wrong about the robbers. He had been wrong about Jeffrey. And now it was going to be hard to act the same way around the man without tipping him off he had figured it out. That was not going to be fun. He looked over.

"He killed someone in the name of magic. He needs to be held accountable." He nodded hopefully.

Chapter 15

The dean's office was rather old fashioned, with the traditional staples: tiffany lamps, a dark wooden desk and a large window behind the desk. It was getting late in the day and the shadows were becoming longer.

Dean Mara Terry turned around. As usual, she had her hair up in a bun and was wearing a very expensive and well-tailored skirt suit. However, he could see the flaking black nail polish and the bags under her eyes—which he guessed were due to last night's Prodigy concert. It was a bit of a public secret that the dean was a big fan of hard rock and punk, but she kept her private life separate.

"You wanted to see me?" Furcifer cleared his throat and looked over to her.

The dean smiled and sat down at the desk.

"Yes. How are you doing?"

Furcifer sighed.

"I'm ok. I'm guessing it's the bangle fiasco?" He asked, sitting down. To him it was a disaster. They still hadn't found the damn thing, and while he was closer to figuring out what it was than he had ever been, it was all just theoretical until he actually found the item.

"It was not a fiasco." Dean Terry looked over him. "You did what you could." Still she wasn't trying to comfort him. He had known her long enough to know that that look was not reassurance, but mostly just routine. Long long ago he had been much more insecure and would have fallen apart much more easily. But he had grown and didn't need such babying anymore. Still, he liked the thought that his boss cared for him. Or gave enough of a shit to pretend she did.

"You didn't ask me here to argue semantics." He looked over.

"No. There has been a new... development. Jeffrey Stone has gone missing."

Furcifer sat up quickly. "Crap."

"You don't look overly surprised." Terry raised an eyebrow.

Furcifer remembered she could usually tell when he was lying.

"Yes... I have been working on the case." Furcifer cleared his throat. "I realised that the bracelet has actual magic, and I am guessing the spell on it actually... It's not active magic, but passive. It's a kind of spell that lays low until someone comes by and activates it." He tried to explain. The dean had never been very savvy about magic so he tried to keep it as simple as possible for her.

She nodded simply. "And from what I read... It would be reasonable to assume this spell has an effect on him?" She asked.

"Yes." Furcifer nodded.

"The empty box of the bangle was found hidden in the storage room about a week ago. Nothing else was out of place... except that the code used to get into the museum's private area was Jeffrey's. He probably didn't even realise, like a force of habit." She followed up.

"So it's pretty certain... oh gosh the implications." Furcifer sat back.

He had thought about them, but it had never hit him this hard before. Jeffrey had committed murder. Had probably lead him astray to distract them. A very horrifying thought.

"So what now?" Asked Furcifer. From the look on Terry's face he could see she'd gotten to the rough part of this conversation.

"I need you to stop your own... research and turn over your findings to the police." She concluded.

Furcifer groaned. "They will not be able to make any sense of them. What do you think they'll be able to do with the study of a spell?" He said with a sigh.

"I don't care. We need to make sure we look like we are cooperating with the police on this." She looked at him and shook her head. "You can keep copies. But really I just need you to stop going after this until further notice."

Furcifer took a deep breath.

"Just... Please know that I had no idea what he was doing. I only recently figured out the magic spell could affect him to this degree."

"So... You should have come to me with that." She said with a sigh. "Now it's moot, of course. There is a warrant out for the police to find him and talk to Jeffrey. If we're lucky you won't be named in the investigation."

"No reason to. I was a good good; good boy." He winked and looked over at her. "Was that all?"

"No. Well. I wanted to tell you you're doing a good job." Terry nodded and looked over him. This was not routine, but actual reassurance. Furcifer was surprised.

"How do you feel?" She continued.

He shrugged. "It's... been different. I don't have the same attention span and I don't have the same patience, but I have a good teaching assistant."

"I noticed. You know your co-workers generally only rely this much on their teaching assistants late in the semester. You know, when they are actually busy."

"I am busy!" He protested. "I am studying the notes I took in India, making courses up as I go and I've been busy with the museum case."

She grinned. "I do know that you cannot leave a mystery unsolved." She said. "Take a few days off. Get out for the weekend and find yourself a new mystery. Figure out if you want to go explore other places after the semester."

Furcifer took a deep breath. "I would love to go travelling again." He had to agree. It had been amazing to see magic used in so many different ways. And he knew there were quite a few factions out there who wanted him if he wanted to leave public academics.

"And get laid." She concluded, getting up and turning to the window.

Furcifer sighed and made his way out of the office. What she said did make sense. If Jeffrey had done such awful things he was not going to be able to go after him himself.

Walking out to the courtyard he realised this was where he wanted to be. His entire life had been about learning and discovery, and he had designed it that way. Still, it somewhat bothered him that he had to let go of the bangle story so quickly. Perhaps he could find a way to get the bangle without even coming near Jeffrey.... The seeds of those thoughts kept him occupied until he reached the tower. Once he reached his books, there were many other things he could find to distract himself.

Chapter 16

The sound of a woman's heels clicked through the auditorium as Manon came in, fifteen minutes late, and continued as she climbed all the way up to find a seat in the back.

"You're late." Furcifer said.

Manon looked down, shrugged, and sat down. With a sigh, he continued teaching.

Furcifer could see a change in Manon. Ever since the last class, she seemed more restless. It had been about a week since he had invited her up to his room to discuss the bangle for the first time, and at first he had just imagined it was because of their disagreement about factions.

Throughout the rest of the class, she had been fidgety, anxious, fiddling with a bracelet and tapping her feet. It seemed... Like she didn't want to be here. Something was definitely wrong. The students next to her seemed to pick up on it as well and either moved away or tried to ignore her completely.

He focussed on the class before him and wound down, a little faster than usual. At the end there were about five minutes left for questions, but his hurried approach did have the side effect that people did actually have questions. He sighed as he gave the word to the first student. Who, of course, had a barrage of questions about the grammar of a proper magic spell. He sighed but let the man ask his questions, from time to time glancing to Manon who was gripping her desk and eyeing the exit.

"But if you are using your hands, you need uh...Two elements?" The student asked hopefully.

"No, it needs to contain three elements. Direction, purpose and length." Furcifer explained calmly.

"But when you do it with, say, a wand, then you don't need length right?"

"NO YOU GIANT FRUITCAKE. THEN YOU DO NOT NEED DIRECTION BECAUSE YOU ARE POINTING A WAND." Finally, Manon caved and yelled, gripping her desk so hard the knuckles were going white.

"How about we leave it at that for today. You can all go." Furcifer made eye contact with Manon as students streamed past him, glad to be out. The lecturer went to lean on his desk and looked over Manon, who was slowly getting up.

"You're not well." He said calmly as he ticked off a few marks on his page of items to teach. "Are you alright?"

"No." She said and walked down the stairs towards his desk. "This damn bracelet – I got it in the mail last Friday. I can't take it off. It's messing with me somehow." She thrust her arm out even though it hurt her quite a bit to do so.

Furcifer took her hand and without touching it, examined the bracelet. He recognised it, but from what? Suddenly it dawned on him.

"What is it?" She hissed through clenched teeth.

"I hope I'm wrong, but it seems to be a bangle similar to the one stolen from the museum." He said calmly, touching the metal with the rubber eraser end of a pencil. "It's definitely got a feel of magic. Fresh magic."

Unlike the item stolen from the museum, this actually seemed to have been recently enchanted.

"No return address on the envelope?"

"You check for those things?" She frowned.

He raised an eyebrow. "You don't before you put on whatever's inside?"

"Uh... I think there might have been. But I just thought it was some kind of online purchase I forgot about!" She shook her head. "I still have the envelope, please, you can have it if you get this thing off of me!" Manon took a deep breath. It was making her feel worse now. Her knees were shaking and she looked like she was about to throw up her breakfast onto the man's desk.

"Just get it off of me! Aiden's shop, Southside Arcade, Zeus City!" She clasped her hand in front of her mouth. "What?"

Furcifer smiled a little. "A spell precaution. The spell came from a friend of mine's... He puts this little tidbit of information in every spell. If someone feels suitably threatened by a spell from his shop, they will suddenly spout that address so they can seek help. So don't worry, the spell is not a malicious one... I think it has just been used maliciously. "

He sat the trembling girl down on his chair, putting his hands on her shoulders.

"Breathe deeply."

He could feel her heart racing, so hard he could just about hear it.

"Now close your eyes. Just relax. Don't think of a single thing. Put your hand on my desk."

"If you're going to saw my hand off, I at least want more of a warning than that." Manon tried to make light of the situation.

"Don't be stupid. I'm not going to saw your hand off. It would be much faster to chop it off." With that, she suddenly heard a loud snip and jumped up.

"What?!" She gasped, pulling her hand back. Her eyes went over the man's form, and then down to the desk. Furcifer was still holding onto the two pliers which he had used to cut both sides of the bracelet, which was now lying broken on the desktop... It was sparking softly, but soon returned to its normal state – as if it was just a normal everyday bracelet.

She laughed a second and then looked at her hand, happy to find it was still attached.

"You're a dick." She gasped.

"You asked me to remove it. Not your hand." Furcifer looked at her and poured her some water from the jug on his desk.

"Have some water." He slid the glass over to her. "How are you feeling now?"

She carefully drank some of the water. "Much better. I'm not feeling like I'm about to puke out my guts anymore."

"That's good." Furcifer agreed and put a hand on her shoulder. "The address you said. It is a well-known magic store in the magic community. If you don't mind, I would like to take the bracelet there and find out more."

A student of his receiving a bracelet with a long-term spell on it? The student who had pointed him at the possibility that the bangle from the museum had such a spell on it in the first place? This was all much too convenient. Something was going on. He doubted Aiden was behind it but the man had been involved in some way and he needed to look into this.

"I want to come." Manon piped up. "I want to know why. Besides, I've never been to a magic store before." She smiled a little. "It'll be fun."

Furcifer sighed. If this had to do with the bangle from the museum, this was risky and he probably should clear it with the dean. In fact the fact that magic had been used against one of his students should probably be recorded in some way... But what good would that do? The student might be banned. His class might be deemed unsafe by worried parents, and through that route, cancelled.

Furcifer got up and cleared the blackboard as he thought about it. Really, he could just put it down as a class trip with a curious student who wanted some more information about magic in the real world. He looked back over to her.

"Well then. Let's go."

Chapter 17

Aiden's store hardly stood out in the arcade, sandwiched between a Build-A-Bear workshop and a candle shop. The mall was located near the more creative part of town, where craft stores and small coffee shops reigned supreme. Women in long skirts and men with woollen caps and long beards walked along the passages of the arcade.

"This is not what I had expected of a magic store." Manon rubbed the back of her neck.

"I'm sure he's still got a zig-zag cabinet in the back somewhere." Furcifer sighed. "Kids these days, impossible to impress." He walked into the store and looked around.

The store was just a heaven to him. The walls were done in a cherry red, with black shelves and a checkerboard floor. The old fashioned style of it attracted him. It had not changed much since opening day – the walls were lined with all sorts of magical items. From beads to fireworks to large pickled jars of things better left unnamed. The counter in the back was wide – almost the entire width of the store – and provided a barrier between the store and the person behind the till. Furcifer knew the design was intentional to keep a divide between his personal and professional life as his own living quarters were just beyond that counter. And it provided protection from any witches who meant to harm him.

Most magic users were fine with the term "mage" being applied to them. Some, however, wanted to be known as "witches", separating themselves from other magic users. They considered their magic to be older, and held a more extreme view than even the Canutta coven which was quite conservative. They felt magic was entirely private and that their modern counterparts were different from them.

Some of those self-proclaimed witches hated mages like Aiden. As a stage magician turned shopkeeper, they saw in him the archetypal mage who could flaunt his magic without retribution, while authentic witches had been burned in the Middle Ages. When his wife vanished, the Canutta coven and the various factions had quickly offered their support and resources, even looking into their own ranks to find the culprits. The perpetrator had not been found, but many suspected the witches.

And Aiden had spent time in jail accused of murdering his wife. Furcifer could see it had changed his once happy-go-lucky friend into a more cautious and reserved man.

Aiden came out of the back and looked over the two visitors, looking quite... cheery. Furcifer frowned.

"Hey." He smiled brightly. "You need your regular supplies? Or did you bring people to help carry more?" He teased.

"We need some information about a spell." Manon shot forward.

Aiden raised an eyebrow. "Well, I'll need some specifics..."

Furcifer rolled his eyes at her direct approach. "He's on our side. Promise. But first... Did you get lucky, Aiden?"

Aiden sighed. "Will you just... What is it you need me to look into?"

"No really, it would be about time you know."

"Not the time nor the place to talk about this, Furcifer."

Furcifer looked over him then shrugged and took out the envelope with the remains of the bracelet. "Do you know anything about this?"

Aiden put on his glasses and looked over the item. "Mmmm... These bracelets are pretty common. Even for sale in this same arcade." He slipped it out of the envelope and onto his counter. "Why are you coming to me with this?"

"Because the girl who wore it... Ah, you tell him." Furcifer nodded to Manon who seemed eager to take the lead here.

Manon stepped forwards.

"Because it was sent to me in a nearly unmarked envelope, then made me unable to remove it. Every time I thought about removing it, it made me sick." She explained, looking from him back down to the bracelet.

"I see." He said, looking over the item. "Does sound familiar. I do a similar spell for tracking bracelets for little children. You know, so their parents can find them easily. To make sure they don't remove them, it just gives them a little bit of a tummy tickle when they try and take it off." He looked up. "I'm guessing it gave you more than a tummy tickle."

"When - when I went to Furcifer to remove it, it almos- it felt like I was going to die. It made me feel so bad I called out your address, which I heard is not a good sign."

"Not at all." Aiden looked over the bracelet again. "I do sell this spell on paper. It's easy for someone to hack it to amplify the effects... Did it have any other effect on you?"

"I don't... I don't think so." She shook her head. "I may have quit smoking." She quipped and smiled a little wearily.

"Do you have a good memory of all you've been doing since putting the bracelet on?" Aiden checked.

Manon frowned. "I uh... The weekend is kind of a big blur. As in I cannot remember Saturday."

Aiden looked a little alarmed. "Then... if you'll let me I would like to examine this further. It seems odd that someone would send you a bracelet you didn't want to take off."

Furcifer cleared his throat. "We – I think it might have to do with the museum case."

"I thought you'd been warned off of that." Aiden almost gave him a reproving look.

"Yes, and I kept my word. I didn't go poking around for trouble... But what are the odds my student was sent a bangle with a long lasting spell on it?" Furcifer raised an eyebrow.

Aiden groaned. "Sounds like you are poking around for trouble."

"You're too careful, Aiden." Furcifer said, though he almost instantly regretted it. Aiden looked far from amused. The shop was the man's safe space, his fortress. To call him out on that was perhaps in bad taste.

Furcifer could understand. Most everyone of those with magic had at one point felt unsafe and searched for safety and security. That was the main reason why some chose to stay with magics – to find that peace of mind they had feared lost when their powers suddenly popped up. Aiden had perhaps been the most carefree of them all until his wife had vanished. After he had been released from jail, he had started this shop as nobody would hire him for anything with a criminal record under his name.

"Sorry." He cleared his throat.

Aiden unconvincingly shrugged it off. "It's fine. Well... – I'll need to look into inventory, see when this spell was bought."

"If it helps, it arrived at my flat last Friday." Said Manon.

"That does help narrow it down." Aiden agreed and flipped open a laptop. "The spell's only been on sale for a month or two. So we have a... seven week window, in which time it has been bought... ten times." He looked up before looking down again.

"It was also shoplifted a once. Huh." He frowned, "That's rare. I mean, people generally find security around here a bit too tight if anything..." He looked up from the screen.

Furcifer sighed. "That leaves a few unknowns... Unless... That night I brought Jeffrey and Russell here, was that one of the dates?"

"On that date... it could have been. I noticed one spell stolen the next day when I did the pre-closing up check. If it really was stolen that night I wouldn't have noticed the same day as the shop was already closed."

"Shit." Furcifer sighed. "He might have stolen it..." He was impressed. That nervous looking man was now ahead of him every step of the way and it was frustrating him. What was he going to do to catch up with him - no. He stopped himself.

He was not going to go after him. He would have to write a report of this and take it to the dean, so she could decide if this should go to the police. He was not going to go after a murderous piece of shit himself. But if the man went after his students... surely he had a reason to try and stop him?

Or he was being drawn out. What if the spell even eluded Jeffrey, and he was asking him to help him here. He had basically just undone the spell. Perhaps that was what Jeffrey needed to know. That it could be undone - to figure out how wouldn't take much longer. Of course he would not have been able to ask Aiden - the man would have guessed something was up. Even so, before all of this... He could have seen Jeffrey simply asking for help.

If the bracelet had warped his mind, perhaps this was his roundabout way of finding out how to escape it.

Chapter 18

Furcifer threw aside another book. Every book he had read offered the same solution to his problem. There was no easy way to do it and there was no way around it.

He had hoped he would be able to disarm the spell from a distance, but it looked like that would be impossible. If the spell was undone, he could just let the police handle the rest. But with the spell in place, with unknown intent... It might encourage Jeffrey to go after whoever came for the bracelet. He got up, carefully moving through the piles of books near his desk, and took his mug to the electric kettle to make another cup of tea.

The fact that he had killed before only proved to Furcifer that this spell was no good. Perhaps it was naive of him, but he was sure Jeffrey would have found a sneakier way to take the bangle out of the museum. It would definitely take longer than just going in and grabbing it, but he was sure he would not have killed. Jeffrey was an academic, not a killer. The problem of pulling off such a heist would be much more challenging than to take the brute force way and just murder whoever stood in his way. And for a museum curator to go murderous over a museum item was hard for him to grasp.

If this case was resolved there was a definite possibility of museum rules being adjusted. They would have to be even warier of unknown artefacts, never allowing anyone to touch them with bare hands until the items had been certified as magic-neutral. It would mean the museum ideally would have a magic expert on their payroll. Not to mention laws governing magic, magic spells and magic items.

He could do that. He would always be an academic anyway.

He quit the daydreaming and returned to the books with a fresh cup of tea. But it was no good. All the books held the same answer: the only way to break the spell was to have possession of the actual, physical bangle. Furcifer leaned back and closed his eyes. If the man was wearing the bangle full time, that would prove to be a problem. Even if he wasn't, it would not be a long shot to assume he would have it under lock and key.

If he wore it... Furcifer put the books aside and quickly went searching for his hurried handwritten notes, made as he was examining the case. They were all gathered in a folder, only because he had had to gather them for the police. After a quick photocopy, they had not asked him for anything more and had returned the originals within one day. He didn't think they had really paid much attention to them, but that was all the better for him he guessed.

He had made extensive notes of the first meeting with Jeffrey. The truth spell he had used that meeting had given him some clues - he had wanted to wear it. If the bangle exuded a spell to make itself be worn... Well that would increase its efficiency. It would just need a low level lure spell, then once it made actual skin contact, the actual magic could come out. It was almost genius.

Furcifer grinned. Whoever made this. He would have to shake their hand. It was so subtle and well done and well... It reminded him of someone he used to know. He closed the folder again and made sure to put it away safely in case he would have to go over these again.

Despite his dislike for factions, he had almost founded one himself. The mage he was dating way back when was ambitious, powerful and eager to start a faction to gather up the research and magic of those like minded ones. He had opposed it and they had ended up breaking up. It was only years ago, but it felt like another life.

For now, he had to figure out whether it was worth breaking his promise to the dean to go after Jeffrey or whether it was best to stay out of it completely and prepare some popcorn while others did the hard work. The one thing he wasn't sure about was whether they would even be able to find him without magic. Jeffrey had proven to be pretty smart on his own, never mind with a magical bracelet that would influence his thinking.

Chapter 19

It had evidently not been a good morning for Mara.

Furcifer still looked half asleep as he arrived at the office, summoned ten minutes ago. His hastily drawn yukata in red embroidered silk made him look more like a wizard than a magic lecturer. His hair was a tousled mess, the curls having free reign as he had had no time to force a brush through. His eyes were almost closed and Mara could swear he was trying to sleep on Manon's shoulder. At least the teaching assistant seemed anxious enough to realise this was a serious matter.

"Atze!" She huffed, putting a mug of coffee down in front of him. "You drink that and tell me why exactly we have the press standing outside our door!"

Furcifer opened one eye. "Fuck if I know."

He took a deep breath and plopped into the seat in front of the desk, freeing Manon to pace around the office. "Also, I don't like coffee."

"I may have a - " the young woman started.

"You know you did something. Just - spit it out!" Said Mara, looking over to Furcifer.

"No, for - ugh! I've just been in the tower, I've not even come near the museum case, just like you asked, and-"

Manon sighed and sat down. "It's not the museum case. Well. It is." She looked around the office. "Do you have a TV here? Or a computer? Seriously, it's been big news."

"Explains why I don't know. I have no TV." Furcifer shrugged and sniffed the coffee before taking a sip. "See, totally innocent."

"We'll see about that." Mara flipped open her laptop and shoved it over to Manon. "What is it?" She asked softer.

Manon tapped in a few keys and opened up a news website.

"Jeffrey... spilled the beans." She said as he took a step back.

Jeffrey looked tired and sad in the video, delivering a heartfelt speech about how he was confessing to crimes committed while under the influence of magic. How he had murdered his co-worker in cold blood just to get the magic he needed. Camera flashes ended the little news segment, which was followed by an article headlined "Former curator confesses murder on fellow Zeus City Museum worker".

Furcifer only sat up straight at an image of Jeffrey extending his arm and revealing the bangle, the so called artefact which had influenced him. Of course the curator himself did not mention the bangle, but the stolen item was clearly visible on his wrist. The museum would know.

"From what I gather... the cops will want to talk to you." Furcifer heard his teaching assistant say. "I mean the museum knows you examined the bracelet, and they'll give that information to the police. They're not exactly known for holding out on the police, and if you're not one of them you're totally screwed." She sighed. "Did a summer job there once. Vicious." She explained.

Mara nodded. "Uhuh...So, the police are probably on their way over. We've already helped them so there is no way there's negligence on our part, but I want the university's barrister with you when you take this interview."

She was calming down now she knew what they were actually facing. Furcifer knew what she was thinking – they went far enough back for that. This could be a good thing for the university if she knew how to play it.

Furcifer read the article accompanying the video with a sense of dread. What was the man doing? This was... well. Not unlike the man he had gotten to know. But at the same time the need for the cameras threw him. What was he planning?

"Furcifer." Mara looked over to the mage. "What is on that brain of yours?"

Furcifer looked up startled. "I'm not sure. I don't know the guy that well... But he's been... pretty obscure lately. I don't know why he's suddenly coming out with his big confession, press conference and all. Also... When I got hit by the car, it wasn't Jeffrey, but they were looking for the bracelet." He straightened up and ran a hand through his hair.

"Really. Don't give me that look. I don't know why."

"What look?" Sighed Mara.

"Like you look at me now. Like I know everything."

"You're the mage one of us two." She shrugged. "Maybe you're like a supernatural being now."

"Yeah. Manon has magic as well, look at her being amazing." He rolled his eyes, ignoring the glare he got from Manon for that.

"Fine." Mara sighed. "So what we know is that he confessed to stealing the artefact and murdering his colleague. The police will be here soon to ask what you know of the artefact, and we will cooperate. So you gather up all you have on it, prepare to give it again."

Furcifer groaned. "Did they throw it in the shredder or something?"

"No, but it always looks good for them to be filmed carrying large boxes of evidence." Shrugged Mara. "So pad that file a bit. Add whatever you found on the spell, it'll look good on us."

Furcifer sighed. This was just the kind of thing he didn't want to be part of.

"Maybe shower, though." Mara said dryly as Furcifer stood up. "Manon, please make sure he showers."

Manon groaned. "Who made me the tamer of that lion?"

"I did. You're getting a pay hike to the level of an untrained lecturer." Mara looked up and grinned seeing the sparkle in Manon's eye.

Furcifer walked out of the office, reluctantly waiting for Manon who was still thanking Mara for the pay rise.

"Come on. We need to get cracking." Furcifer sighed. "Also, keep an eye on this story. I want to know what happened." Something didn't feel right. The whole time Furcifer had seen the man being one step ahead. There was no way he was just giving up like this. Something was happening. He didn't like that thought.

Chapter 20

"You know, if you'd waited with shredding my findings a week longer, we'd be saving a tree here." Furcifer sighed and looked over. His tower room was filled with people moving boxes, gathering papers.

"And if you were to digitise, we could maybe get this place clean." Manon sighed as she looked around all the notebooks, stacks of paper, actual books and just random scribbles that took most of the space in Furcifer's tower apartment. She cleared a seat and sat down.

"Why should I when the police will just mess it up anyway again?" Retorted the mage.

"Yeees... The cops caused this mess." Manon shook her head with a sigh. "Totally not the giant slob who lives here."

"Do you want to pass your exam, Manon?" Furcifer ended the bantering.

"Ma'am! Did you hear that!" Gasped Manon before looking over to Mara, who was pinching the bridge of her nose.

"Yes, I did. So would you two behave, please?" She pleaded. This was bad enough without the two of them just bickering like little children in front of the police officers.

The officer in charge of the search raised an eyebrow. "Just making sure we have everything for this case as well." He said, looking through the photocopies that Furcifer's newly installed scanner and printer spewed out. This was to avoid a fuss with uniformed cops taking materials out of the man's room and to the photocopying centre. And as the writings technically belonged to the university, they could not just take the originals.

Furcifer sat back and sighed. This was the second room raid in as many months, and it was starting to get old. True, he had added to the data he had on Jeffrey. Like his use of the truth spell and the fact he seemed to be ahead of them, and his suspicion that Jeffrey had killed the curator. This knowledge could get him into real trouble especially as it looked like this time they might actually read what he had written down.

To use magic on an unwilling human was bad enough. To possibly withhold information about a murder would be obstruction of justice, or in the worst case, a criminal matter. It wouldn't be a long shot to assume he was in league with another user of magic. Especially as he was secretive and hard to track. Had spent time abroad without having checked in with the university on a regular basis. Ironically, the real crime he did commit was unknown to them: publishing knowledge the university legally owned.

Even Manon hadn't found that one out, and the young lady was in his tower almost daily to help him out with classes. Bringing him the photocopied tests for the next day. Marking the tests from the day before. Dumb things that he could handle himself if he just thought they were important in any way.

"Right, that's all we need right now." The police officer picked up the box of copies. "Thanks for your cooperation. Don't know how much we'll need of it now that he has confessed"

"Sooo glad you came and wasted my time for that then." Furcifer snarked and got up. "I bid you good day, gentlemen!" He walked them to the door and sighed.

Once the officers had cleared out, only he, Manon and Mara were left. Finally, some peace and quiet.

Mara crossed her arms and tapped her arm. "Furcifer. Anything I need to know?" She had noticed his vacant look.

"No. Okay, maybe I used a truth spell on Jeffrey at the time. And I was suspecting that he had masterminded the theft... I didn't know much more." He shrugged.

"Atze!" She groaned. "That's bad. Is that in the notes?"

He cringed at her use of his first name.

"I write down everything." He simply replied. "There's no better way to forget than to just write it down. You should try it."

"If his lawyer finds that out – that you used a truth spell...." She groaned. "They can argue that the confession won't hold and they'll come after you next."

"For what, dubious research methods? There's no law against using spells. Except maybe in Salem." He raised an eyebrow. "I did nothing." He glanced over to Manon. "Maybe she shouldn't be here."

"Yeah, but you have the warm tower room with good gossip and I have a lot of grading to do." Manon looked over. "So I'm staying put." She gathered her grading work.

"What were we even talking about again?" Asked Furcifer.

Mara threw her hands up. "I'm calling our barristers." She sighed and walked to the door. "Manon, please keep him out of trouble for the time being."

"I make no promises!" She said, taking a deep breath. "But I need to do some work anyway." As Furcifer shot her a glare, she gulped and focussed back on the tests she had to grade.

Chapter 21

Furcifer sat back. It had only been an hour since the dean had left his living quarters, and he disliked it. At last, even Manon had nipped out to go get some coffee, which meant he was finally alone. The smell of books was overpowered by the smell of other people – colognes, hair products... He opened up a window to let some air in and looked out the window a few minutes. Suddenly, he felt the hair on the back of his neck stand up.

"Gabrielle." He slowly turned around.

She was a stately, muscular woman. Long silver hair and a strong face, dressed in a chainmail top combined with a pair of jeans.

"Furcifer." She calmly replied, looking over him. "Travelling has done you well. You almost have a bit of colour in your face."

"You hit me with your car." Furcifer raised an eyebrow. "What do you want?"

"Just to talk." She smiled a little, her hips swaying as she closed the distance between them.

"And that was just to make sure you didn't have the bracelet already, that would have been dull... I have been looking for you. Missed you." She reached out and stroked some hair from his face.

Instinctively, Furcifer moved into her touch before pulling himself away.

"Doubt it." He said. "Did you put him up to this? The human?"

"Jeffrey? Hmmm... Jeffrey the human... Does ring a bell." She tapped her chin as if deep in thought. "Oh yes! He picked up something you were supposed to find. Well. I left so many of those little bracelets around. They're only activated when found. I was hoping you would find one first." She sighed and took a step back. "You haven't missed me?"

He sighed. Oh, he had. She was one of the few who was on his level when it came to magic. They had spent long hours talking, debating, inventing spells together... It would be an understatement to say there was history between them. They had shared entire worlds and built new ones together.

But factions grew. And he had not wanted to become a part of those.

The witches had been one of the first. They were a disorganised group, with only strong morals to make them a group. From their more liberal offspring, the Canutta coven had come about. They were some of the oldest and best organised groups, with their own schools, universities and living blocks. They had grown into exclusive societies, which people with magic could know about, but never join. Usually the populace would know that they were expensive and elitist, but they would not know they were aimed towards mages.

Then there were the ones like Gabrielle, who deemed themselves alike gods. Who thought they had been chosen by the power they wielded. Furcifer disagreed. If there was one thing he knew it was that he was just another stupid human who had just... gained a power. A gene that was activated, somehow. Maybe by age, maybe by a spicy chili, but certainly not ordained by some higher power. She had felt that they needed to grow their own faction, separate themselves from non-magical humans and only allow magicals who had learned one spell on their own into their coven, much like they themselves had had to learn everything from scratch.

Obviously, this was a point Furcifer disagreed on. There was nothing special about any of them. There was no gain in letting mages let their powers go to waste because they couldn't fathom how to fashion a spell. Especially when nobody had a clue how anything worked yet. To him, it was the high point of elitism and the catalyst for his first spell book. After publishing the book, he'd been expelled from the coven.

"Just drop the spell book nonsense, my darling." She flipped one of his note books closed with a smile and took his hand. "We could be as one again. As we were before."

He closed his eyes, remembering. It had been a beautiful time. She had understood him as no other.

"No." He finally sighed and pulled his hand back. "You let go of that human, Jeffrey. You're the one who made him kill."

"He is a useless wannabe!" She hissed. "He did not know one spell before I came to him. Not a single one!"

"That doesn't matter!" He raised his voice somewhat. "With or without magic he is a human being."

"Do you care so much, Furcifer?" She leaned against his desk. "Then come back to my faction. Stop writing your useless books. Stop sharing your knowledge with the unworthy."

"The unworthy do have money." He looked over to her. "You cannot control this. Magic is chaos. You cannot faction yourself off and pretend it works. It will only make the humans hate us."

"Who cares!" She got up and looked over him. "Let them come after us. We have magic."

"And they have guns and fifteen humans to every mage we have!" He looked over to her. "You're an idiot, Gabrielle." He closed his eyes.

"I'm giving you an ultimatum." She crossed her arms and flipped her hair over her shoulder. "You rejoin us. I let go of Jeffrey and take all the bangles I scattered back. I will erase everyone's mind about the murders. He'll just think he went on a bit of a bender."

"And what if I don't?"

"Well, it should be an entertaining trial. And once that is over, it's only a few years before the next artefact shows up and makes some silly human my puppet." She pushed herself away from the edge of the desk. "Think about it, Furcifer."

Furcifer turned around and could hear the vanishing spell that took her away. He could save the boy's life. Jeffrey would be able to go back to his house, annoy the hell out of Russell and start a new career.

Furcifer looked around the flat he had. All of this he would have to give up - teaching, writing, most communication with non-mages. He sighed and closed his eyes. It was a tough choice, no matter how you looked at it.

It came down which group he wanted to belong to. The ones dedicating themselves to magic and nothing else. Or the group which actually got out of the house and talked to well-rounded, general purpose people without magic from time to time. While it would seem the first option would be the one to go for, he was unsure. There was only so much to learn within a closed group of people weary about who joined them, and who seemed to think themselves better than even other magical factions. It seemed the harder it was to join, the better.

Furcifer plopped down onto his bed. He had to admit that he did want her end of the bargain. If she could sort it, then he would definitely be able to do the same. A wide grin appeared on his lips.

Gabrielle's proposition was to clear the boy of all guilt, erasing the minds of the people he had confessed to, and to remove all enchanted bracelets which had lead up to this situation.

He could do that.

For Jeffrey, that was the barrister's problem. He could help out a bit, destroy the bracelet and let the boy get his wits back. Once that was done, he could... flip some switches in people's brains using magic. It was a simple enough spell. Attach a little worm of a spell to the name of Jeffrey, with the simple effect that people forgot what he had confessed to. Paper copies were easy enough to destroy. Computers tended to malfunction.

The bracelets, well that would be harder. Without knowledge of what they looked like or how many they were it was... needle in a haystack like work. To do this on one's own would be impossible... But there was more than one mage in his class. He could... what did the students call it? Crowdsource it. He chuckled.

It could be done. It would be hard, but it could be done.

Perhaps he was an optimist after all. Too much time among non-magical people, perhaps. He picked up his cup of tea and retreated to his kitchenette to make a fresh cup. He needed to do some thinking right now.

Chapter 22

Furcifer had been up most of the night, trying to figure out how he would do this. First and foremost, however, he needed to know who could be counted on and who would help him in this crazy plan of his. After some phone calls, he had everyone gather at Aiden's shop.

Manon arrived first, holding a cup of coffee from the Starbucks a few doors down. She took off her sunglasses and winked at Aiden. Furcifer merely rolled his eyes.

"Not going to work out, Manon." He reprimanded her.

Twitch came in second. "Hi!" He grinned. "Oh, hello." He looked to Manon, who just gave him a little wave. They vaguely knew one another from class, but hopefully they would get on enough to make this work.

Finally, Russell showed up. When Furcifer had called him to see how he was coping with the whole thing, he seemed alright. Russell had even said he would love to help his house mate out, so while he had no magic to speak of, Furcifer had invited him anyway.

"Sorry I'm late... It's uh, kind of different to find this place without beads..." He scratched the back of his head and looked over to Aiden, who cleared his throat and looked away.

Furcifer raised an eyebrow.

"Wait, you two!" He took a deep breath. "Aiden, you were married, to a chick!"

"So?" He shrugged. "You were rolling without magic once, but you happily rode the track to become magic tsar. Things change."

"That's different! I'm not perverting my own students."

Manon sighed. "I'd say you do worse sometimes."

"You are growing a backbone. I am not sure I like it." Furcifer glanced to Manon, who just shrugged.

"What's this about, Furcifer?" Russell cleared his throat and tried to get them back on track.

"This, we're discussing this later." Furcifer wagged a finger between Aiden and Russell, before finding a seat central to the store. "Alright. I uh, found some information. It seems a lot of what happened to Jeffrey ties back to me."

"An asocial mage with a big ego attracting drama? No way." Quipped Manon.

"What did I say about that backbone, Manon?" Furcifer glanced to his teaching assistant. "Now, the why's and who's are rather unimportant."

Manon crossed her arms. "As someone who has been targeted by whoever this is, I tend to disagree!" She said, looking over to him. "So you say what you have on this person."

Furcifer sighed and looked over her, pretty much knowing she wasn't going to let this go.

"Alright. She... and I used to be a thing, way back when. She was my best friend when it came to magic. There were very few people who had it back when I first got it. She...wanted to set up a society for magic, one that would promote knowledge and things like that."

"You mean a faction." Twitch sighed.

"How do you know about those? It is what it... turned out to be I'm afraid." Sighed Furcifer.

"Hopeful faction." Twitch looked over.

"Twitch the hopeful. Interesting." Grinned Furcifer. The Hopefuls and the scribes were semifactions closely related to the Elites, which was one of the biggest factions. They acted as collectors and archivers for the Elite. There was only one difference: the Scribes were solely focussed on gathering and sharing their information. The Hopefuls, through study and practice, sought to improve their magic enough to join the Elite.

"Anyway, don't let me keep you from telling your tale." Twitch said.

Furcifer reluctantly came back to his story. "Fine. I left her faction to go work for the university and she made the faction even stricter in the admission rules." He looked over.

"Soo...?" Sighed Manon, not quite getting why he was dwelling on this.

"She wants me to join again." He sighed. "The bracelet was a lure. I think she lost track of me while I was abroad."

"So you're telling me... She put that bracelet somewhere to influence someone to murder a curator, and then - she's coming for you?" Manon raised an eyebrow.

"She knows I care. That's the issue. She offered to let the kid go, undo all she did to him... if I joined again."

"Oh gosh. Fuck that." Manon looked over. "Just - join her or whatever, then! I mean come on. You can't let a guy go to jail because of a stupid ex!" She threw the hand not holding a latte up in the air and looked over to him.

"She would not let me leave." Furcifer said seriously. "Not to be a dick or anything, but I'm kind of needed out here. So I don't really care what you think. I'm not joining some secretive faction that won't let me share what I know."

"So the university will have to find another lecturer." Sighed Manon, annoyed she seemed to be the only one who was speaking up. She glared around.

Russell took a deep breath.

"It's not just the lecturing, is it?" He asked, looking over. "That spell book I found of yours... It had the same kind of structure as those secretively published spell books have. You produce those." He looked up to Furcifer. "Does the university even allow you to publish that stuff?"

Furcifer sighed and nodded. "I will vehemently deny it if you ever tell anyone else this... But yes. I wrote those. The university doesn't know about them."

"Then... Appoint someone else." Manon looked over to him. "Someone else can do your job. You seem to be under this impression that you cannot be missed. I do most of your job anyway."

Furcifer sighed. "Look. This is not what this is about!" He huffed. "Don't just... dismiss this. I know I'm a dick. But I want to make this work. I want to - I want to help Jeffrey, okay?"

"But what if you can't?" Manon asked. "It's a tall order to do what you just described. We would have to prove magic was behind it." She said and took a deep breath. It would be near impossible.

"But it could be done." Furcifer looked at her. "Come on." He looked over to the lot and stood up from leaning against the counter.

"It's near impossible." Manon sighed and looked over. "We'd need to prove his innocence-"

"Or erase some minds." Furcifer said. "That's how she said she would do it."

"Some minds." Twitch nodded. "You make it sound so easy."

"You have an entire Faction which could help broadcast a signal. It would need to last only a few seconds. That's all." He looked over. "Just... Make everyone believe he was not arrested for murder and that he did not confess. He just had some outstanding tickets and needed to appear before a judge."

"That's... a big worm spell." Twitch shook his head. "I don't know if it would work."

"It will." Furcifer said. "Don't worry."

"So then... You need to find how she controls him." Aiden nodded.

"It's the bracelet. The bangle he stole from the museum. I think he's the one who sent one to Manon – so it's possible he's already figuring out how to undo it himself. However I don't want to count on that." He said.

Aiden sighed. "So we need to snip that off of him – hang on. If he was arrested that bracelet would have been taken from him already, together with his personal belongings."

Furcifer sighed again. "Perhaps he doesn't need to wear it... But that makes it even harder. If we can't get to the bracelet it's near impossible to break the spell. That's the entire weakness of the spell – It depends on the enchanted item and how easy it is to break."

"So if we get him out then we need to make sure we get this bracelet off of him and... destroy it?" Russell took a deep breath. "I could do that, I guess. I mean I'm not going to do any big magic but I can snap a bangle in half." He sighed.

Aiden nodded. "That's your deal then. Cause once we start doing this, she'll react. So uh, stay in contact with Aiden... That shouldn't be hard."

"This is crazy, Furcifer. You know that, right?" Manon sighed.

"Let's call it your final project for this course." He had long found out grades motivated her more than anything. As she perked up he knew he had given her the right incentive. Figuring out how to make it fly for tor the dean would be small fries if they pulled this off.

He looked around. Russell would do it to help his friend, and Aiden would do it because he was a good person. Perhaps that was why Russell and Aiden seemed attracted to one another. Both of them were good people who wanted to do the right thing.

"If anyone does not want to help with this, you can leave now." Furcifer insisted. "No consequences. But if you stay I need to be able to count on you." He looked from one to the other.

Manon's eyes fluttered to the door for a second before she sighed.

"I'll help." She put a hand up. "I can... help with the mind erasing spell or something. It's a very specific one, it'll be very long. Two people minimize the chance of errors."

Twitch nodded. "Thanks. It'll be useful." He said.

Russell nodded. "I'm in."

"I'm in." Aiden sighed. "I'll provide any necessary materials." He looked around. "How rude of me. Did anyone want a cup of tea or coffee?" He asked, as if just realising there was a gathering in his store.

Furcifer chuckled a bit. "I think we're about to go home, anyway." He patted Aiden on the shoulder. "Thanks for letting us meet here."

Aiden shrugged. "Not a big deal. If you give me a heads up next time I might be able to have some coffee or tea ready for you guys." He opened up the front door of the shop. "Come on, get out of here." He sighed as people started leaving.

Furcifer was the last one to move. "Aiden."

"Yes?" The mage looked over the man.

"I'm not sure I can do this." He admitted, now that nobody was around.

"You're trying. You're at least not giving up without a fight." Aiden put a hand on his arm.

"Do or do not, there is no try." Sighed Furcifer. "If this fails I have to seriously consider either joining her or letting the boy rot in jail."

Aiden took a deep breath. "Let's focus on this first. If this fails you can start panicking about your evil faction." He tried to make a little light of the situation.

Furcifer snorted. "You just worry about your own. You and Russell, huh?"

Aiden chuckled. "Look... He's just a guy and -" He looked over to him. "We hit it off one night. Doesn't mean anything."

"Just saying. It's been a few years, you can... Start looking for someone else now." He grinned a little. "You deserve to be happy."

Aiden sighed. "I'm not looking." He crossed his arms. "Now get out of here." He nodded towards the door.

Furcifer grinned knowingly and walked towards the door. "Alright, alright." He halted just a few steps away from the exit and absently looked over some candles.

"Aiden. If this doesn't work..."

"Don't give me that. We've been over this." He said.

"If I join her again, I mean." Furcifer turned his head towards him.

"I know." He said. "I've kept my CV updated but you haven't given me your letter of recommendation for the university yet." He mocked a little, hoping to relieve tension.

They had always had this kind of pact that if one of them vanished, the other would take their place as best as possible. If Aiden vanished, Furcifer would try and keep the store open, as it was the only place in Zeus City for magic implements. If Furcifer disappeared, Aiden would try and curate his knowledge and try to collect more as best as he could. Furcifer especially was well aware both of them were the cornerstone for a very small scene.

"I'm surprised you didn't ask Twitch." Aiden added. "He seems gifted."

"He seems young. And he's in the Hopeful faction. They might impede his work. You, my friend, are as objective and neutral as they come." Furcifer picked up a candle. "I'm out of these. What smell is it?"

Aiden chuckled. "Pine with a hint of summoning power. Go for the lavender with the relaxation spell built in."

Candles with spells were relatively easy – the wick contained the spell which was slowly consumed by fire as it burned. For some reason, it worked. Aiden always tried new things which meant he could often bring out innovative spells.

"The purple ones? They look atrocious." Furcifer groaned.

"Take one free or leave it." Aiden sighed. "Do a man a favour and he complains about the colour of it!"

Furcifer chuckled dryly and picked up a purple candle. "Thanks, Ai."

Chapter 23

Twitch walked into the large apartment building most of the Hopefuls lived in. It had been bought communally, and was used to set up both new and older members who preferred to stick close to the main administration.

While the building looked grey and stern from the outside, Twitch couldn't help but feel like he had come home as soon as he stepped inside. There was a lot of magic in this place. The inside upkeep was mostly done with magic, though any works relating to utilities were done by handymen. The inhabitants themselves, however, loved tinkering with plasterwork, beams and anything else that they could fix magically.

As he walked down the hall towards the elevator, he smiled to Jeanie, one of the oldest residents in the building. The old little mage gave him a little wave and a smile, and he narrowly avoided being pulled in for cookies and a glass of milk. It was nice though - this was much like the village he had grown up near.

As he walked down the cheerily painted hall he looked around. Some kid's drawings had been hung up, and a few even had dared paint on the walls.

A young lady with honey brown skin, her hair pulled back, was standing in the doorway of the last apartment. She was talking to an older woman in a long dress - Twitch recognised her as one of the elders.

The young lady was the new leader, Mary Rosen. She had risen through the ranks due to her exceptional powers and her speciality in restorative magic. Yet, she was not one to underestimate just because she stuck to white magic. She possessed a quick tongue and good wits. And while she did not like Twitch, they got on decently. They just didn't mesh - his values were very medieval and she was very much a modern woman.

"Twitch." She smiled a little, seeing him back. "Been a while. How's university going?"

"Just a few weeks." Twitch returned her smile. "It's been interesting. I'm happy to be back, though."

"I'm sure you are." Mary nodded. "You sent that you wanted to talk some business. Let's go to my office." She led the man up to the elevator and pushed the button for the top floor.

Twitch took a deep breath. It would take like five minutes to get all the way up there in the old elevator. He had better get the small talk going.

"So how has the faction been?" He asked, hoping to banish the silence. The elevator could really do with some music, he thought as he peeked around.

"We're doing alright." She nodded stiffly, a tell tale sign they were not. There was a pressure from the Elite to merge with them rather than stay their own faction. Meanwhile, there was a fifty-fifty split within the faction about whether they should stay with the Elite or become a faction of their own.

Twitch just decided to nod politely and waited for the elevator to reach her office: a spacious room with a beautiful view of the city around the building. A bit lost on a woman who couldn't see past her own nose, honestly, but he would not bring that up. He merely cleared his throat and sat down.

"So?" Nodded Mary.

"I'm sure you've kept up with the situation of Jeffrey?" He started. "The man who claims to be influenced by a magical item?"

"Ah, yes." She sat back. "Got what he deserved, if you ask me. Messing around with that kind of thing."

"See thing is - he didn't... He uh, was attracted by the bracelet." Twitch tried to explain.

"And?"

He took a deep breath. This would be the hard part. "Me and my professor are devising a plan to help him. I would need to request the power of the whole coven for a spell to help prove his innocence."

"We're not helping out a mage whose quest for knowledge has driven him to ruin." Gabrielle walked into the office. "Oh! I'm sorry. I don't think I've met you yet. I am Gabrielle, head of the Elite Faction. We're fully merging with the Hopefuls to bring out the best in each faction." She smiled proudly, pacing to the middle of the room as her heels clicked. Twitch blinked and looked over to the woman who looked every bit the power woman in a finely tailored black long skirt, a matching blazer and a blouse peeking out from under it, almost in the same gray as her hair.

"You're fully merging?" Twitch looked up.

"In a way. The Scribes will be an introductory Faction, offering membership quite freely, even to Hopefuls who are not selected to join the Elite. The Elite will take in any with exceptional talent." Mary nodded.

Twitch shivered. The Factions would become solid entities this way – especially when the Hopeful Faction went into such a deal. It would drain the talent out of the Hopeful faction and leave the learners to only receive morsels from the Elite. Moreover – it could lead to knowledge being pooled rather than shared so the Hopefuls could record it. But if this was the Gabrielle Furcifer had spoken of, then they stood to gain a lot of knowledge getting Furcifer back among their ranks. This move had happened to make sure Furcifer could not resort to this group, currently the largest, for help.

Twitch slowly got up, wary of the woman's fixed gaze upon him.

"I'm sorry to have wasted your time, then." There would be no use talking to her now. If anything, it could give Gabrielle more information.

"Sit down, Twitch." Mary said, looking over him. "You're with this faction by my grace. My predecessors allowed you because of the great effort it took the mages to revive you. You're nothing but the side effect of a spell by naive old women."

"Maybe." Twitch said. "But I am the one they chose to bring back." He took a deep breath and resisted the urge to sit back down. His history was well known to all in this faction.

"Aaah... You are the Twitch I keep hearing about. Asa Ward." Gabrielle gently picked up a file and started reading through it. It seemed the quick movement of her eyes over the paper matched the pace of his heart. "Well. Explains a few of your phobias...." She looked over to him then continued to read.

"Brought back to life by a group of mages testing a revival spell. The spell is only partly known to the Faction and is currently being researched by the few survivors of the spell and a small group of dedicated Hopefuls."

Gabrielle smiled as she closed the file. "As I expected. Furcifer didn't want to ask for help himself, knowing how massively disliked he is, so he sent his happy little sidekick." She pushed him back into the seat and looked over him. "What's his plan?" She asked.

Twitch looked away, not answering. He was outraged his coven was selling out, calling themselves a faction. He could guess why. The faction would die out eventually the way it was going. Forming a faction with the Elites would make sure they had a future.

Twitch startled as he heard the sound of a match being lit up. He could smell the phosphorous chemicals of the match burning up.

"Tell me." Gabrielle's calm voice resounded as she leaned in with the match.

Twitch gasped and blew it out, looking up to her with beating heart. "Mary..." The woman had spilled the beans about his greatest fear.

"Tell me." Gabrielle circled his seat and her footsteps caught fire as she walked, creating a circle of fire. Mary looked away as Twitch whimpered, curling up in the seat to try and escape the flames, though he could already smell burning fabric. His hands frantically patted to put out the edge of his pants, which had caught fire. His eyes watered.

Gabrielle just leaned against the desk and with a movement of her hand, raised the flames so that they were now about a meter high. Twitch screamed and tried to curl up tighter, feeling the smoke in his throat already. The memories of his death rushed back – the sight of the heat hovering over him, the smells of fabric and skin burning. Worst of all, the pain.

"Tell me, Asa, and all this goes away." Gabrielle said.

"He is planning to free Jeffrey and break the bangle!" He screeched out, sobbing. His hair had caught fire and he was trying to put it out, feeling the heat all over his body once again. "Please! Stop this!" His shirt had now caught fire and he was screaming, his throat hurting from both the effort and the smoke.

Gabrielle put out the fire.

"Put him in a room. We might still need him." She walked past the shivering, terrified mess Twitch had become and out to the elevator.

Mary stood up and picked up Twitch easily. Twitch didn't really remember much of that – he passed out seconds after the fire went out.

Chapter 24

Furcifer entered the classroom, looking around the faces of the students. Shit.

No Twitch there. Ever since he had sent him off with his little assignment to get help from the Hopefuls, he had not seen him anymore. Hopefully, he was okay. All that he had heard was that the man had sent a summary note that he was dropping out. He didn't believe a word of it.

But he blamed himself. If he had gone with him – there was a bigger chance it would be denied, but at the same time it would have been safer for the young mage. A large part of the plan had now fallen apart. Even if they could somehow get Jeffrey out... It would be an escape.

There was little else to do. He would have to talk to Gabrielle. He reluctantly returned to teaching the actual class he had come in here to teach, letting the class take the lead with a debate about magic rules. After giving the three fundamental rules of magic, he had let them to debate on what rules they would add or remove, and what kind of laws would have to be put in place.

"Mind control." Manon piped up after raising her hand. She shot Furcifer a defiant look.

Furcifer looked up at her. "Explain." He simply said.

"Rules against mind control, along with a proper way to prove mind control as a crime. Otherwise it could be used as an alibi constantly."

Furcifer sat up straight. If they could somehow prove that Jeffrey had been manipulated...

His writings, writings that the police had, already mentioned the effects of the bracelet. Impulse, mind manipulation. It could form just the seed of a defence if he could speak to the man's lawyer. Of course, with him being under Gabrielle's control it was possible she had made him refuse one.

In which case he could just force one upon him. He grinned and sat up.

Again, Manon had brought in a fresh idea.

"So kids, no homework today. Do rehash, you might have a pop quiz soon!" Furcifer got up and dismissed the class, keeping Manon back. She merely glanced at him, adjusting her shoulder bag and slowly walking down the stairs of the auditorium to the professor.

"You're smart." Furcifer told her. "You didn't seem to be too enthused about our plan though."

"Because it's stupid. You've already been hit by a car. Where's Twitch gone since you sent him off? I think he just ran off. That he came to realise this plan would not work and took off to safer pastures." She crossed her arms.

"I hope so to." He admitted. "But now that Twitch is out of the plan, we need to find a new way to prove Jeffrey's innocence.... By proving he was being controlled."

"Good luck." She sighed and looked over him. "The only way you could do that is if you had some proof this bangle influenced him before all this." She couldn't help but think about the bracelet she had worn for a bit. Too bad she had not made any notes about it – getting it off was a bigger emergency at that time.

"I might have. It was originally a case I was on – the director asked me to vet the bangle for possible magic, which is how I met Jeffrey. It was clear then the bracelet had an effect on him." Perhaps if he had identified it sooner. Perhaps if he had realised... Jeffrey would not be in this mess.

She sighed but uncrossed her arms. "Fine. You think you can prove that thing influenced him, compelled him to do it? Good luck." She turned and walked away. "Just –" She sighed and didn't finish her sentence, though she pointedly looked at Twitch's desk before leaving.

Furcifer sat back down. He had understood the hint - she worried about Twitch. He did the same, but Twitch was a grown up. He knew how to handle himself. Or so he hoped at least.

Furcifer sighed. He was in charge of this crazy plan and he needed to think up an alternative. The route they were going with was not working out. Manon had brought up a good point and he would have to follow it up.

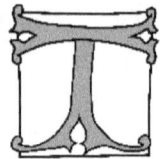

Chapter 25

When Twitch woke up, he found himself in one of the top floor apartments. He was still in his same clothes, but his phone and other items had been taken. His hair still smelled burned.

He curled up in the bed he had woken up. Fuck. Without the Hopefuls, Furcifer didn't stand a chance. He would probably be okay as long as he cooperated, but he also had no way of letting Furcifer know the plan was compromised. He rubbed his hands together in an attempt to a communication spell, but it did nothing but warm his palms. The room probably dulled magic to keep him here.

The apartment itself was pretty standard, much like the one he had lived in until he had gone to university. One bedroom, a small lounge, a simple bathroom and a well-furnished kitchen. He wandered around the small space, trying to figure out what to do. His bare feet were grateful for the soft carpeting, and the rooms were warm and familiar, but they still felt like a prison to Twitch. It was probably Mary's intervention which had netted him a cosier cell, but it was still incarceration.

Mary. He had known she didn't like him, but to betray him like this? Gabrielle had her well under her thumb. From what he had found out, Gabrielle was a powerful one. Even more so, she was smart. She had given this faction something they badly needed – a way to stay alive. In a world of factions, loose groups like theirs could not exist. It was adapt or die.

On a whim, he tried the front door and found it securely locked, the keyhole having vanished from the lock. Cute new trick, he thought. But if he was going to have to wait to get high enough on Furcifer's list of priorities, he would be waiting for a very long time.

A letter slipped through the mail slot, after which it securely snapped shut again. A letter from the university.

Twitch sat down on the floor and ripped it open, surprised to see the date shown being three days later than the day he had come here. He had been out for that long?

Dear Mr Ward,

We are sorry to hear you are unenrolling from our course for this year. As requested, your refund has been processed and will be in your account soon.

Thank you for considering us.

Shit. They had unenrolled him from the course, ensuring nobody would be looking for him. Maybe his fellow conspirators would, but Furcifer would probably dissuade them until they had reached their goal. Three days had passed and Jeffrey would be closer to his trial date.

Maybe the plan had completely failed already. Jeffrey would go to jail for something he had been forced to do. There was no way to prove he hadn't done it. Twitch slipped down to sit and lean against the door. Damn it.

Suddenly he jumped up, trying the wall mounted phone.

"Yes?" Mary's voice came.

"Oh, hello operator. I'd like to make an outside call." Though his mood had dropped severely hearing her voice, he hoped to make light out of it.

She snorted. "Nice try. Pick up the phone when you need anything." She hung up, leaving him with a dial tone.

Well. That hadn't worked. He suddenly realised he was quite hungry and walked to the kitchen. To his relief, there was no gas stove. The electric hot plates were workable. He put a pot of water onto one of them and turned it on. As the heat built up, his hands started shaking and had to turn it off. It took him a few minutes to get himself together again. Finally, he walked to the phone.

"Yes?"

"Can I get take out?" His voice was still shaking a bit, and he cleared his throat. "Whatever. I'm hungry." He said. He wasn't sure if her silence was pity or not but he didn't care. Right now he was frightened of a slightly warm pot of water on his stove burning him.

The other end of the line was quiet for about ten seconds, which seemed an eternity.

"Pizza okay? You like pepperoni right?" She finally said.

"Yeah." He hated that his voice still shivered as he said that. "And uh. Some chicken wings. And maybe some – sides. I'm really, really hungry." And he could use them as leftovers for the evening. Or whenever his next meal would be. The clock on the wall showed about six pm.

"Of course. I'll bring it to you as soon as it arrives." Mary's voice sounded soft, but she hung up straight after that. She obviously didn't want that to be used, which made sense to him. Gabrielle had probably warned her not to do anything stupid.

He slid back against the wall and sighed. Shit. He needed to get out of here. Moping, however, would not help now. Slowly but surely, he got up again and started testing the weaknesses of his little cell room. There were none. Papers had been written in this faction on how to contain magic. And while those had been aimed at containing uncontrolled magic from young, inexperienced mages, the same could be used here.

He walked to the lounge and looked around. It was his own room – he recognised the leftover books. Some adventure novels, some history books. He had enjoyed reading up about history.

Twitch's own history was peculiar in more ways than one. It was drenched in magic.

During the middle ages, his family was gifted in magic, especially on the side of the men. Usually they had a natural tendency towards white magic and restorative magic, which meant most people did not fear them. In fact more than one villager back in the day had come to him and his family asking about a cure for some silly ailment that was easily cured.

But then the witch hunter people came to town. It had been a bad harvest, and people were already restless about the coming winter. Food supplies were running low, and then these rich, fat people said that their misfortune was caused by witches. For a low one-time fee, they would point out and eradicate the source of this misfortune once and for all.

They were fat and boisterous, so the townspeople had to assume they were right. Didn't look like any of their harvests had failed recently. When the witch hunters pointed at the Ward family, there was some difficult swallowing. At the same time there would be an entire family less to feed, people who lived on the edge of town anyway, and who knows? Perhaps these strangers were right.

Twitch remembered little of what had followed. It had been a long, painful while filled with wet dungeons and guilty, pitiful looks until he had been "Convicted" of being a witch. While they were not technically wrong, he did disagree with their way of punishment.

It was at least over soon. He vaguely remembered the flames, but even the memory would cause him to burst out sweating, hands shaking. He still feared fire to this day.

And that's where his story would have ended if it wasn't for a coven of ambitious mages a few decades earlier. Henrietta and six other Hopefuls had set out to prove that death was not final, that it could be reversed. The wealth of information it could bring.... It had made the risk worth it. However, only three of the seven mages who set out to revive him had lived, and the spell had been hidden away. To this day it was one of the most lethal spells ever performed. The mages responsible had been banned from the coven, a hard enough punishment. Twitch, not wanting to be a burden, had moved away. It wasn't until 1977 that one of the Hopefuls found him and wanted him to join the faction. After years of being alone in a world he did not understand, it was a relief, and he had joined eagerly. He had bought into the agenda and had worked hard, so one day he might be considered for the Elite.

How all that had changed in a single day. What had been a peaceful, loving faction had been turned into something corrupted, twisted. Twitch shook his head and pulled out a history book to read while he waited.

Chapter 26

Furcifer hung back in the classroom, looking, no, staring at the empty seat left by Twitch.

Yes, he knew that Twitch was an adult, and while he would never admit it, he suspected the man was more powerful than he himself was. But that sudden notice that the man was dropping out was disquieting.

Of course the dean had asked him not to look at it like some sort of disappearance. She saw people drop out every day, whether they just lost interest or could no longer pay for it. Twitch was strange enough that she didn't need to think up a reason. Furcifer didn't trust it, however. He knew Twitch lived at the university, but his unenrollment meant he would have been asked to move out within 48 hours. He would go and see if the man had already moved out since.

He slowly got up and sighed. It would take a detour past the dean's office to find out the man's address – and he didn't think he would get it by asking nicely. He would have to break into her documents and find it himself.

It was now eight pm. By now Mara would have gone home, or so he hoped. He looked around the empty classroom once more.

It was back. That feeling where he knew every face in the classroom, knew every name and quirk. And the strange feeling of caring for them. Stupid. He was feeling for a bunch of people who could hardly be bothered to roll out bed to come to this classroom. Okay, perhaps they had more in common than he cared to admit. He snorted at the thought and walked up to the main hall, looking around.

It was about as empty as he had expected it to be on a Friday night. Even the cleaner seemed to have made short work of it – the floor had been hastily wiped and mopped, and he could clearly see dirt in the skipped corners still. He slowly made his way up to the dean's office.

It was locked. He muttered a spell and the lock popped open, giving way. He walked in and closed the door behind him quietly. While the cleaning lady might have skipped on her duties on the lower floor but here, people tended to be a bit more diligent. It was a well-known fact the professors would slip the cleaners a few fivers once in a while to clean their rooms as well. It was a strange ecosystem.

Come to think of it, it hadn't been that long since his time abroad and he had done the same thing just today to make sure his newly tidied room would be dusted a bit. The cleaning lady had taken the fiver, glared up the stairs, and had turned around. Whether she would actually do the cleaning remained to be seen, but he remained optimistic. He sighed and peered around for a filing cabinet, opening it up. It wasn't locked. The flimsy cabinet lock had broken long ago and usually the office door could keep people outside well enough. He rifled through it until Asa Ward's file popped up.

Less than a minute later, he was out of the office and on his way to the dormitories.

Even if he found nothing, it was better than sitting in his room, overthinking Twitch's disappearance. This fool's errand was at least keeping him occupied. As he stalked across the campus grounds, he tried not to think about the worst case scenarios.

Typical Friday night – students nervously smoking outside. One student puking up the last two pints of alcohol they had chugged. Two sitting out on the lawn having a philosophical discussion, thinking nobody else had ever done this besides them.

He'd seen it so many times. And he hoped he would see it many more time – it was such a perfect mix of people, budding into better people either by finding people who were as good as them, or by being so utterly stupid they would vow to do better next time.

It seemed like Twitch's corner of the campus was quiet. There were no parties going on in the dorms there. Except for one or two lit rooms, everyone seemed to have gone to bed already. It was almost jarring considering the mess of people he had just walked past.

The dorms were all small rooms, set up much like stacked containers with staircases leading to a second floor if there was any.

Twitch's room was supposed to be on this second floor, so he carefully made his way up the slippery metal staircase in the dark before knocking on the door.

No answer. With a sigh, Furcifer wondered if he should go so far as to commit burglary twice in one night. He peeked around and then forced the lock open magically, before stepping inside.

It looked uninhabited. The floor was scrubbed clean, and there was no sign of anyone living in the small unit. The kitchen was completely empty, the kitchen chair stacked on top of the little plastic table. The door to the bedroom was wide open, but there was nothing there. Not even a forgotten soda can. He sighed and walked out, closing the door behind him. Whoever had done this had made sure not to leave a single trace. With just the moonlight shining, it was almost eerie. Almost a small ghost town.

Furcifer could see Twitch making a home out of this place. It was small, cosy and modern, and most of all it was high up. Twitch seemed to be of the old fashioned mage class which believed that the higher up you got anywhere, the more your powers were amplified. Furcifer had always dismissed that theory as simplistic. From what he had found there were more factors that influenced magic than just how high up the user was - there was age, talent, language, even some research that pointed at certain genes playing a role.

Twitch, however, was not here. That was a bit of a setback. The next place where he suspected the kid to be was the coven. Unfortunately, it was a bitch to get into if you weren't a member. From the intel Aiden had sent him on the coven, they were pursuing the title of faction.

Gabrielle showed up in town, a wizard disappears and suddenly the Hopefuls aim to form a faction? Things had to be related somehow.

He sighed and walked back to the more lively part of the university. The sounds and lights proved both distracting and reassuring after the eerie silence of the dorm.

"Hey!" Manon called out. "Furcifer!"

Furcifer looked up with a frown. His student was sitting around the bonfire area - a large stone circle within which students would light small fires to smoke around and warm themselves up. The woman was sitting between two young ladies who were passing a beer between one another.

"Manon." Furcifer nodded and looked over. "You uh. Have company."

"Oh! It's cool. This is Diana and Emily. Diana, Emily, this is Furcifer, my professor of magic." Manon filled in the silence where she had expected Furcifer to introduce himself.

"He usually never misses an opportunity to brag, so I would say to enjoy the silence." She quipped as there was no answer from the mage.

"So you do magic and shit?" Diana asked, a short chubby girl with red hair and a rather stoic face.

"Yeah." Furcifer sat down near the three.

"I don't believe that stuff exists. It's like smoke and mirrors, right?" Diana added, her eyes keeping to Furcifer.

Furcifer raised an eyebrow and muttered a spell before pointing at the fire, which briefly flared up green. "Oh yes. So many mirrors round here." He said sarcastically as Diana scooted back a bit.

Manon looked over to Furcifer. "You look tired." She said, noticing the man was slumping a bit.

"Yeah, no shit." Furcifer straightened up. "It's fine. I'm just about to head to my room." He sat up. "Don't worry. Magic won't hurt you, Diana, was it? The people who use it could."

Diana shivered. "You're really weird." She said.

Manon looked over to her. "Don't worry about him. He's just... He's a professor, you know how they are." She wanted to make sure the girl didn't run off and not insult her professor at the same time. Quite the balancing act. Furcifer snorted a bit.

"It's fine." He simply said and looked up. "It is weird." He straightened up and looked over to Manon. She was so carefree, so unlike him at this moment. While he thinking about how to get Twitch back, here she was, just having a beer with two attractive girls. They even seemed to be somewhat into her, as Diana easily returned to her side and leaned her head onto her shoulder. Manon's arm easily returned to embrace the girl. They were adorable, and even Emily stuck close to Manon.

Furcifer sighed. "I need to go." He said, getting up. "Get some sleep." That was a pretty universal fact among university dwellers - needing sleep and being excused for it.

"Yeah. I should get to bed too, I have an early class." Manon straightened up and sighed. "Can I walk you two to your dorms?"

"Nah." Diana shrugged. "We're going back to the party." The other girl just shrugged and followed her lead. Diana leaned in and kissed Manon's cheek, before taking her friend's hand and taking off.

"You totally would have had a chance with them." Said Furcifer as he looked over to Manon.

"Maybe." She shrugged. "There'll be other opportunities. And Diana kind of put me off."

Furcifer remembered how insecure Manon had been when she had come to him, saying she missed home. Having someone think negatively about magic was not a nice thought.

"There will always be people like that, you know." Furcifer said softly. "Even if it's not your choice, some people will."

"Like homosexuality?" She perked up.

"No. Oh God no let's not go with that trite comparison. Gays have been around for ages, we just got here ten minutes ago in comparison." However, just like black people had supported the pro-gay movement, there was a likelihood of the LGBTQI+ community coming to their defence when they came out in full force.

He just hoped that wouldn't be necessary. It was already crappy enough without the civil rights bullshit.

"Like you would even notice." Smiled Manon. "You just sit there up in your tower with a good job and no need to worry about girls or getting employed."

"My last girlfriend turned into the head of a cult which is threatening to put an innocent in jail if I don't join her." He shrugged. "So I don't think that comparison hold up very well."

Manon looked over and laughed. "There's that." She shrugged.

"Trust me, kid. I'm older than you. I've seen things. The factions might even be a good thing one day. They make us look organised and well regulated."

"That why you don't want to join one?" She asked as the sounds of the party grew fainter.

"No. It's because I value objectivity. Factions may look great when we're talking non-magical people but outside of that, it's just a warring shit show. Factions might compete among each other to snap up new mages, get positive exposure and show their members just how damn good they are." He sighed. His feelings on the subject were mixed, to say the least.

Manon nodded slowly. "I guess."

Furcifer blinked. Usually Manon never gave in that fast, but he guessed students had a way of feeling like they needed to say what their professors wanted to hear to get the good grades. Universities were as old as time, but they also bred a certain culture, a certain way of looking at the world. Jump through these hoops and we give you a fancy piece of paper.

Maybe factions would be good. It would give them a possibility of bringing people together, who could work together to solve the giant gaps in knowledge that were there. But even those plaids of knowledge would be useless if they couldn't be brought together into a single tapestry.

There would be no grand prize for gathering all that knowledge – but they would lose if they did not.

Manon looked around as they walked. "Oh! Furcifer, I need to head this direction." She said. The path they were on forked here, and she needed to take the one branching off to the right to get to her dorm.

"Okay." Furcifer thought a second then looked over. "I'll walk you home."

"So, why were you even out so late?" Wondered the student, looking up to Furcifer. It was already getting colder. She pulled her shrug closer around herself.

Furcifer sighed. He had not told anyone what he had gone and done, did he?

"I went to check on Twitch's room."

"And?"

"It was empty. Cleared out. Not a trace." He shook his head.

"Oh." Manon actually stopped in her tracks. "That's... No good." She said, looking back to Furcifer. That was very, very bad. There was no way Twitch would have packed up and left like that. His attendance record was spotless, he turned in homework before anyone else did and had some of the highest test scores. There was no way this was something voluntary.

"I know." Furcifer added, walking along the path. He actually looked tired. His shoulders were slumped and his usually fierce looking eyes seemed to droop.

Manon sped up her pace a bit. She suddenly didn't feel very safe anymore. The sooner she would be in her room, the better.

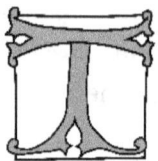

Chapter 27

Twitch chowed down on the newly arrived pizza. It was deliciously hot and he was hungry as anything. He had a tendency to get bored easily - to the point where he had been praying earlier. The concept of God had become a little harder to believe in with all that had happened to him, but he was still raised as a good Christian. It gave him comfort to rehash the familiar Lord's Prayer.

"Mary? You still there?" He asked, after having almost inhaled the first slice of pizza.

"Yeah." Mary said hesitantly. She was about to take off after having slipped the pizza through a portal into the room.

"You should have some of this pizza with me. It's amazing."

"No thanks. It's got meat." She wrinkled her nose, but sat down by the door.

"Oh yes, I forgot! Sorry." He said. "So want to have a cheese popper maybe?" He asked.

She hesitated but then opened the tiny portal again. "Alright, just one."

Twitch slipped the box through halfway so she could take one.

"Thanks!" She said as he pulled the box back.

"Thank you." He simply said. "I'll pay you back for this. Or just take a twenty out of my wallet, I know I've got plenty of stuff lying around in storage..."

"Dude. How can you just..." She sighed. Her captive was offering to pay her back for the take out. How absurd.

"I'll get you some fresh clothes."

"I can, Mary. Because I believe you're thinking you're doing what's best for the faction. You're not. But as long as you're not hurting anyone, I will not mean you any harm."

She shivered at those words. He knew more spells than any of them. If he decided to use those against them... He could just make them all mute. Render them immobile and freeze them. She had seen the notes they had made about him - especially when he had just been resurrected and had been full of hate. Henrietta had told stories about how he had almost exterminated a campus of people in Salem for re-enacting a witch burning. Even after being convinced it was not real, he had made everyone on campus unable to see for a whole day. Albeit a temporary state of mind for the man, she had seen some real hate and rage in those eyes she had not seen since.

And she hoped never to see them again.

"Anything you need besides clothes?"

"No." He simply replied, sounding like he had his mouth full of pizza. "Wait. Mary?"

"Yeah?" She got up and brushed some crumbs off of her skirt.

"I forgive you. But know that there's a limit to what anyone forgives." He said softly.

Twitch really did believe what he had just told Mary. He'd lived with them all for a while and they had been good people, nice people. They all tended to stick to themselves for various reasons, whether they had been booted out by family or did not believe they had much to share with the world. But he had seen a good soul in each and every one of them.

Gabrielle, however, was different. She was like Furcifer, and him, seemingly out of place. Someone who had been... pulled into this time and place for some reason. He remembered the young girl whose appearance had suddenly changed when she had gotten magical powers. Her powers had been great, but she had no more insight in her magic than any regular mage.

Furcifer was out of place because of his appearance. Most people in the street could not see past it, and it was easy to see he was one "of them magic folks". Maybe that was why he hid in books and magic, to find where he belonged. To find a reason for his transformation and test the limit of his powers. To help others who had woken up, changed like he had.

Or maybe he was just a self-obsessed dick.

Chapter 28

Aiden cleaned up the shop a bit, happy to close up for the day a little early. He checked the till quickly as Manon swept the floor to help out. It was considerate of her, but from what he had learned she had not wanted to stay with Furcifer after their disagreement.

Manon had come to him after speaking to Furcifer that morning. While she was no longer upset with him, she had hoped he would be a bit more careful now that Twitch had vanished. She said that he didn't seem to listen to her – to her claims that they could not go on with this stupid plan without Twitch. He could see she was blaming herself – she would pause from time to time, leaning on the broom and thinking.

There was no use trying to change things after the fact and he knew that better than anyone.

"Hey. Less moping, more mopping." He said to her.

"That's the worst." Still, she smiled a little at the pun. "You're old enough for dad humour, congrats."

"I'm not that old." He shook his head. Though sometimes, he did feel that old.

After a cursory till check, he turned the keys in the store door's lock and flipped the sign to 'closed'.

"So what have you got for me?" She turned back to him.

Aiden unrolled a map on the counter.

"Right. Evidence lock up is pretty much in the police precinct where the suspect is held initially until it comes to a court date. Those are locked up tight. Luckily, personal belongings, not so much." He ran his finger from the drawn entry to the building to a room with lockers. "That's where everything is kept in marked boxes. You need to find one with Jeffrey's initials."

"So how do I get in?" She looked up to him. The route from the entrance to the locker room was pretty straight forward. Getting past the cops would be a different matter.

"Well. That's the tricky part. You've watched Harry Potter?"

She scoffed. "Of course."

"We're going to use a potion."

"You're kidding." Her eyes widened with disbelief. "Like the one that turns you into someone else?"

"Well. It's not that of course." He straightened up. "But that would have been cool. No, too many variables. What I've got instead..." He put a little bottle on the table.

"Notice-me-not." He went on to explain. "It keeps you from being... noticed. People will see you but then promptly forget to do or say anything about it. They'll forget you even existed after a second."

"So I take that-"

"We take that. Until I hear from Twitch himself that he's a-ok and just got distracted by a cute girl mage or whatever he's into, I don't want anyone in this operation doing anything on their own."

"I like that." Manon had to admit, looking relieved that she would not be on her own. Ending up like Twitch... vanished without a trace... That was not a nice prospect. He looked up to her. "Come on, focus." He made sure she focussed on the map again.

"How long does it work? The potion thing."

"Three hours. But be careful, the first hour it will have the same effect on us, so we've really only got two hours." If they both went in then promptly forgot about the other... that would be useless.

"Okay... That should be enough, right?" Manon looked up and bit her lip.

"Yes. If we go straight in and out we can do this in fifteen minutes. I've been inside this police station, it's pretty small. Just remember the layout well and don't get lost." He looked at the map.

Manon had to admit he was very good at this reassuring thing. The longer he talked, the more manageable this task seemed. She looked over the map and memorised it as best she could.

"We find the lock up, grab the personal belongings with his name on. Find the bangle and haul ass out of there." Aiden said. "That'll be the best way to do it."

Playing it safe was his biggest priority with this. Not just because of Twitch's sudden disappearance, but also because of his own past. He had been arrested before and being found breaking into a police station would not help that at all.

She nodded. "So we take this, chill for an hour, then realise we're not alone and go to the station. We make our way straight into the personal belongings locker, grab the bangle and run. Can't we just destroy it there?"

"No. It might be evidence of what Gabrielle did. Besides, if we can analyse it and figure out how it works, we could reverse the effect. The bangle you had might have been completely different. There is no way to tell if simply destroying it is going to help in any way."

"Ok... And what if the bangle is in evidence already?"

"It won't be." He said simply.

She nodded. "You're the man with the plan and experience. So, let's do this."

Aiden grabbed two glasses and poured some of the bottle into each glass. "Now remember. You will feel like I'm not here, at all. Just... Take it easy and make yourself at home, I guess?" He took a deep breath and drank his own portion.

It worked almost straight away. Manon's presence was... there. But he couldn't quite focus on her. It was as if she was just someone on the street. It felt like she was a customer, the kind where he could immediately tell they had just come in to waste some time, looking around and then leaving without a trace again. There was no way he could - he couldn't even remember her name. Huh. He retreated to the kitchen and made dinner, vaguely knowing there were two of them.

He made pasta with courgettes, a simple dish he enjoyed making and which basically involved stewing garlic and courgettes until they formed a sort of sauce, before mixing it with pasta and cheese.

The smells of the garlic eased his nerves a bit. It came back to him that he was going to have to do something quite dangerous soon. Well. They would not be breaking into the police station but they weren't supposed to go there either. Especially not to mess with a suspect's belongings. Luckily, the two of them had no connection to Jeffrey, so it would make things a bit easier. Worst case, if they were caught, they would be accused of being thieves rather than people who were actively obstructing an upcoming trial.

The drained pasta steamed up the kitchen tiles a bit, and the sizzling of the garlic and courgettes broke the silence. As he mixed the two components together, he didn't even think to set the table. Why would he, if he was all alone?

When the pasta and sauce were mixed and he had served himself, Manon nodded over to the bowl.

"Can I have some?" She had to focus to get his answer.

"Sure." He said with a shrug. "There's plates in the cupboard on the top." He pointed and then twirled some pasta around his fork.

"Thanks... Whoah. That's really far up." She looked up to the cupboard, which was hanging about a metre above her head.

Aiden nodded at the plates and one seemed to slide down and into her hands.

"Magic means my house doesn't have to make sense." He shrugged. It was a common problem for mages. Cohabitating with others without magic was hard as they had a tendency to use magic to organise their house, which made it impossible to be in any way practical for those who didn't have such powers.

She put some pasta onto her plate and sat down, watching him eat at the counter.

He was such a bachelor. However, he had once had a wife. Someone who had cooked for him and had taught him the basic recipes he could now cook by heart.

After the meal, Manon put the plate into the sink and looked around for Aiden. This time, he could lock her eyes on her.

Aiden looked over to her. "It's been about an hour. Can you look into my eyes?"

She sought out his eyes and nodded. "Yeah. That was just really weird." She snorted.

"Well, never mind that" he grabbed his coat. "We have a bracelet to steal."

He nodded and walked towards the door, wondering just how many times that thing would be stolen and found before all this would end. It was getting somewhat silly.

The police station looked much like any police station. Not very welcoming and not a good place to hang around. However, they were still going to go in and try to find this damn bracelet.

Manon was the first one out of the car, adjusting her hoodie and resisting the urge to put her hood up. Aiden simply walked up to the entrance as if the whole building belonged to him and walked in. Manon sped up to catch up with him, grabbing his sleeve.

"Slow down."

"I just want to get this over and done with." He whispered back as he made his way past the reception desk. The clerk there briefly looked up, then looked back down to the forms he was filling in. Obviously he didn't feel they were much of a threat. Their footsteps hardly made a noise as they walked past officer after officer, but hardly anyone even looked up.

Aiden had to admit he was relieved. Someone with magic might have been able to sense them, but it seemed the station was pretty much mage free. Not for the first time he realised he himself was using magic to bend the rules and would probably be contributing to laws being set up to avoid this kind of abuse. It was very likely he and Furcifer would be the first ones to be approached to represent the mage community and here he was, breaking into a police station.

Oh well, best not to dwell on it. He had to focus so he could keep himself and Manon safe from any harm.

With a sigh he made his way to the holding office and peeked in through the little window.

"It's clear." He opened the door and slipped inside, briefly holding the door for his partner in crime. Manon wasted no time in joining him, and looked around the room.

It was just row upon row of filing cabinets, which were only locked with the standard filing cabinet latch.

"It's locked!" Manon gasped as she tried it.

Aiden gave one a brief touch and the latch opened up without protest. As he pulled it open he checked the boxes inside.

"Right. This is A - so it should be over... there." He counted a few cabinets out and made his way to the one where he expected Jeffrey's things to be.

"This is too easy." Manon chuckled nervously.

"Well, what did you expect? Fort Knox? The police has no reason to suspect these things would be targeted, except maybe by other cops..." He paused and looked up, wondering if there were security cameras. He didn't see any. If there were, they would be hidden.

"Keep looking." He said as he moved to the wall near a plug, and put his hands on it. He closed his eyes.

He could feel the electricity moving in the wires behind the plaster. If he focussed, he could tell where it went. First one he followed came out into a lightbulb, as he expected. The second one lead right down to the plug. The third – that was the one he was looking for. He moved gingerly in the direction of the current and found the camera, hidden behind a grate.

"Looks like they did feel there was reason to be careful."

"How did you...?" Manon looked confused.

"No time to explain now. Did you find it?" He asked, opening the grate so he could get at the camera. Electricity related magic was rare – hence why he had studied it. He had a little bit of natural talent for time magic, but never used it due to the complications. Even a few seconds worth of shift could mess up a lot of things. Due to his reasonably useless main talent he had sought out other fields to excel and electricity magic was one of them. He touched the camera and easily sabotaged the last few hours of footage, replacing them with a loop of the same time the day before.

"Found it!" Manon tilted the bracelet out of the box and into an envelope.

"Great. Time to go." Aiden replaced the grate and hurried out of the room with her.

Manon walked out first. They still had about half an hour to spare, but she seemed eager to be out of the restricted area sooner rather than later. She put her hands deeply in her hoodie and walked back to the entry hall, hands running over the envelope and making sure it stayed closed. She didn't even look behind her as she made her way out. Aiden saw gain speed, causing him to lag behind.

"Aiden?" She frowned and looked around, somewhat panicked.

"I'm here." Aiden walked out a moment later. "Seriously, sweetie. No need to panic." He put a hand on her lower back as if they were just a couple getting lost in a city.

"Everything okay?" An officer walked up to them.

"Yeah." Aiden smiled his charming smile. "I just told her to come wait for me at the police station if we get separated." He didn't volunteer more info. It was the mark of an accomplished liar to be so smooth. He had been in prison, targeted by other mages... So it was no wonder he had learned to keep his head down. She smiled vaguely to the officer.

"Come on, I want to go to the shops before they close!" She tugged Aiden's hand, and the man smoothly followed behind her.

"You're a good liar." Manon remarked.

"Not by choice." Aiden shrugged.

"Still, it's a gift." She grinned a little, putting some distance between her and the police station. "Holy shit, we did it." She breathed out, releasing some of her tension.

"Yup." He laughed and looked around. "Let's go for some coffee, not go straight home." He said. "So, how's having Furcifer as a professor working out for you?"

"Ugh." She laughed and shook her head. "The homework is terrible. But it's... interesting. He didn't go half as deeply into the material as I had hoped but I guess he had to keep the course entry level. It does mean some boring classes from time to time. But it's good overall."

"Why did you enrol anyway?" Aiden looked over.

"Well... I want to be a social worker and I'm guessing over the next few years more people with magic will pop up. Which will also mean teens with magic running away from home, or homeless magic people. It helps to have that edge, that knowledge you know?"

"I hadn't taken you for the compassionate type."

"Common mistake." She shrugged and looked around for a coffee shop. "That one looks affordable and cop-less enough for my tastes." She grinned and walked towards the little cafe.

Aiden held the door open for her. The little coffee shop had a smooth music radio station playing, and smelled of coffee and baked goods. The sounds of ceramic cups and chattering immediately put her at ease as she walked to find a table.

"Want me to get the drinks?" Aiden suggested.

"Yes please. I could do with a hot chocolate." She sighed and took her coat off, draping it over a chair.

Aiden nodded and made his way to the counter to order a latte and a hot chocolate. He peeked back to the girl, nervously trying to focus on her phone. She was just a kid. He shook his head. She was holding up well, but she was inexperienced. He was just glad it was over at this point.

It was not right to use her, but they had nobody else, sadly enough. Right now they needed all the manpower they could get, even if that did include college students. At least she was in some kind of training – enough to know about magic and its effects.

He sighed and took the drinks when they arrived. When the bracelet was back in the shop they would have to study it, make sure it was the same one Furcifer had studied earlier, before destroying it. It would be no good to them if they destroyed the wrong one then fooled themselves into thinking it was all solved.

Aiden set the hot chocolate down in front of her. "There. Relax a little." He tried to smile reassuringly. "You did great."

She glanced up and returned an uneasy smile. "Easier said than done. I can't believe we just – did what we did." She stopped herself just in time.

"I know." Aiden sat down. "If it helps... We didn't hurt anyone. If anything, this will help someone who is innocent." He stirred some sugar into his coffee and sipped it.

"We did a good thing. Perhaps in a slightly controversial way, but still."

"That's one way to put it." She chuckled and stirred her hot cocoa. "It's... strange. You grow up with the whole – *listen to the policeman* – and all that... and then one day you realise it's just... tripe."

"Welcome to college." He said, perhaps more condescending than he had meant. "You're an adult now. There's a lot to learn out there and not all of it is pleasant." He said, hoping that would help a little. "Also, not all you've learned is tripe. You just learn to discern what is actually necessary for your survival and what is not. What rules can be broken and which not."

"Next thing you know you'll be telling me Santa isn't real." She snorted as she sipped her hot chocolate.

"You'd be surprised what is and isn't real." Shrugged Aiden. There had to be at least one magic user out there who fancied himself Santa. And if that man or woman thought of themselves as Santa, and went out and brought gifts, who was to say there was no such thing as Santa?

Chapter 29

Furcifer could hear banging. He frowned, looking around for the source of the sound, but couldn't find it. He looked around for the source of the sound. It kept going, even though there were no doors to be banged on. Twitch. It had to be Twitch.

Suddenly, his eyes shot open. A dream. He'd slept in, and the banging was at his door. Probably Manon to tell him he was late to class again. He sat up and sighed, unlocking the door with a spell and a hand wave.

"What?"

Manon rushed in, eyes glancing over the man in the bed.

"Uuuh..." She cleared her throat and looked away from the man. The sheets were a tangled mess between his knees, not a stitch of clothing on him.

"Oh grow up, Manon." He pulled the blankets up. "What is it?"

"It's – Me and Aiden went and got the bangle." She held up the envelope. "Uh, magic doesn't work through paper, right?"

"Give me that." He snatched the envelope out of her hands. "Are you sure this is the one?" He peeked in, but immediately recognised it.

"Right. It is the right one." He nodded and took a deep breath. Shit! If they broke it, hopefully that would release Jeffrey from the control... However, that would fix little. It wasn't even sure he was being controlled still now that the bangle had been away from him for quite a while. For all he knew, they would just be destroying museum property.

But hey, a bit of anarchy had never hurt anyone.

"I'll handle it." He put the envelope aside and sat up. "You did good, though." He nodded and looked up to the girl.

Manon nodded nervously. "That's what people keep telling me. Just... fix that."

"I will. I will bathe it in a special potion to remove all magic, make sure it shows no more signs of it, then destroy it." He promised.

"Thanks." She got back up and sighed. "It's almost... anticlimactic. Not a single police car outside my door to take me to jail."

"Careful what you wish for." Chuckled Furcifer. "Go on. Go to class." He wrapped the blankets around his waist.

"So... That Gabrielle... You think she will leave him alone now?" She asked, not quite moving away just yet. She needed to know that this was almost over.

Furcifer wondered if she wanted a reassuring answer or the truth. Unfortunately, he was just going to give her the truth.

"Yes. She put him where she wants him and unless something changes, that's where he'll be. She has no further use for him at this point." He said and walked to the bathroom. "Thanks for bringing me this. It means... He may have a chance." He said. If he did snap out of it, that could mean he came to senses about admitting murder and his defence would have an actual shot.

She scoffed and shook her head. "You're shit at being reassuring." She walked out and closed the door behind her. For her, the hard part was over. No matter what happened, she could happily say she had done her best to help the man.

Immediately, Furcifer leaped up and started on the potion. If they were lucky, it would start working as soon as the bangle hit the fluid. Worst case, it would need a twenty four hour soak. Luckily, the ingredients were pretty straightforward. Purified water, charcoal and a few other ingredients. Magic wasn't always just magic. There was also a part of chemistry in it, though nobody had quite figured out why some ingredients worked as they did. He had some vague ideas how it worked – the charcoal acted as a sort of filter to make sure the water was as pure as it could be to help the magical reaction from the other ingredients. As soon as his potion was ready, he poured it into a bowl. Then he opened the envelope and slowly slipped the bangle into the solution.

No bangs, no hisses. Merely a quiet plop as the bangle hit the water.

Furcifer took a deep breath and retreated to the shower to get his thoughts in a row. It had only been seven thirty when Manon delivered the package – no doubt she had wanted to drop the package off on her way to her first class. He turned on the shower and watched the water run for a bit before getting in.

This had been a crazy week. Things had gone so fast ever since he'd started this stupid plan, and now they would hopefully finish it. Without Twitch, there was no real way to launch the earworm spell that would convince people Jeffrey was innocent. Hopefully, the man had a good attorney, because they were about to destroy the only evidence he had been controlled. He worried briefly whether they had made it worse, or better. With a shake of his head he entered the shower and washed up. Life went on, and he had classes later that day. He had to hurry if he wanted to finish destroying the bracelet before he needed to rush to class.

Robe securely tied around his waist, he left the bathroom.

Gabrielle was leaning against the windowpane, flicking through his notebook.

"Such knowledge, Furcifer. You are writing on the magical properties of some of these Chinese teas... Very insightful." She paged onwards. "Aww! You have a drawing of me."

"We were once to be married, Gabrielle." He carefully took the notebook away from her and put it down. "What do you want?" He asked.

"For you to join my faction, that's all I've been wanting. I've joined the Elites with the Hopefuls. It's beautiful, Furcifer. They're all so talented." She smiled, proud of her achievement.

"I found a way to beat you." Furcifer said defiantly.

"You found the bracelet. But it's not going to help. I'm done playing though. I'm done giving you and your minions the time to go behind my back. So I'm calling a deadline." She pushed herself away from the window and walked over to him.

"Again?" He sighed, looking over her.

"You decide. Here and now."

He smiled. Did this mean the bracelet had stopped working already? There could be no other reason she had gotten here so fast. He looked over her face, trying to find the tell-tale giveaways that she was hiding something, but there were none. Perhaps she had upped her poker face since the time they were together. He hoped not, as this would be the worst possible time for that to happen.

"No." Furcifer said, though he still could see no indication that she was lying.

Her face tightened as she looked over him. "I don't think you meant that one through properly, Furcifer. Take your time."

"I think you lost your hold on Jeffrey, and that you're trying to push this through while we think he's still under your command."

"Bullshit." She barked, a tell-tale sign he had caught her off guard.

Furcifer breathed in sharply. If she didn't know about the bangle, that meant she did not do this for the reason he suspected. Or maybe she was playing him. It wouldn't be beyond her.

Furcifer whipped around and grabbed the bowl with the bangle in it.

"We stole this. There is no way you still have a hold on him." He thrust it out towards her.

She peeked into the bowl and raised an eyebrow. "Bold. You went and did that? No, you sent in someone..." She grinned. "Someone impressionable who would do anything for you. One of your students." She smiled and turned her back on him. "Perhaps I'm barking up the wrong tree. I bet Manon would be much more suited to join us."

"Don't you come near her" hissed Furcifer, grabbing her arm.

She turned back around with a smile. "Oh, did I hit a nerve there?"

"What did you do with Twitch?"

"Ah, yes. The other one you sent in to do your dirty work." Gabrielle tapped her chin and pretended to think. "Gosh! Can't remember for the life of me. Put him away somewhere and forgot. What happens, Furcifer, when you run out of people to fight your battles for you?"

"You want a battle?" Furcifer took a step back and opened his arms as he felt his anger flare up. "Let's battle. Winner decides the outcome of this whole mess."

"Gladly. I know you'll lose." She smiled and rubbed her hands. "Mage's rules."

"Mage's rules." Furcifer nodded. No blood would be drawn, though these fight usually ended with a large amount of bruises. The fight would work in turns so magic spells did not aversely or unexpectedly hit each other, creating unforeseen side effects. It wouldn't be the first time two spells had bounced off of one another and hurt a bystander. The fight would continue until one of them ran out of magic power or spells.

Furcifer had wondered why she seemed to have taken to wearing chainmail lately. It couldn't be practical and it definitely wasn't lightweight attire for today's modern woman. There was no way she could fear being stabbed that much. Soon, however, he realised why. The long chainmail sleeves acted as a sort of conductor, allowing her to send a spell any direction just by pointing her arm, as if she was using a wand. It made her spells quite a bit shorter and faster to fire off. This she readily used to start the fight, sending a small fire spell in a circle around him.

Furcifer had no wands, so his spells were longer as he needed to direct them verbally. Still, it was better than walking around looking like a generic wizard.

He jumped out of the circle before the flames grew too big, and put them out with a simple wind gust spell. He was definitely at a disadvantage here – without a staff or wand he would have to spend slightly longer on each spell, and they wouldn't be amplified as they wouldn't pass through a conductor. Easy enough to figure out what he should target, then.

Furcifer immediately launched back a spell, making her chainmail ten times heavier and thicker.

Gabrielle hissed as the sudden increase of weight pulled her down. The larger rings made it harder to move, especially her arms – it was becoming hard to keep them high enough to launch any spell. The asshole had found an easy way to impair her abilities... She clambered back up and launched another spell at him, arm trembling with the effort.

The stone floor of the tower suddenly became quicksand, drawing a hold of Furcifer's feet and unbalancing him.

"Just evening out the playfield." She winked and looked over to him.

Furcifer hissed but spread his legs a little to steady himself, before quickly following up with a second spell.

Furcifer, however, felt a lot of the rules didn't apply in this situation. It was a matter of life and death for the man in prison right now.

He sent off a freezing spell, which she narrowly dodged, only to be hit in the shoulder by the second one.

"You cheat!" She gasped, clutching the wounded arm.

"That's rich coming from you!" Furcifer howled.

She hissed and quickly shed the chainmail, staggering away from him. Then, with a deliberate throw of her arm, she threw a bolt of lightning with her good arm. Furcifer dodged it, but it fried his electric kettle. As it sparked he winced and jumped away from the explosion.

Furcifer took a step back. He knew her. Being wounded would mean she would fight less predictably. They circled each other. Furcifer tried to read her, but there was just anger and determination.

There was a tense silence for a few seconds, before there was a loud bang at the door, making the mages jump.

"Furcifer!" Manon's voice sounded almost muffled through the wooden door. Good. That thick door would help keep her safe.

"Go away!" The last thing he needed was to draw someone else into this battle, especially when it looked like Gabrielle was about to unleash hell on him. Her eyes were fixed on him and she grinned demonically. Wounding her was probably making her more dangerous than anything he could have ever done. The door creaked open and Furcifer looked up.

"I told you to get away!" He glanced over at Gabrielle, who had already raised her hand to cast the next spell. Furcifer dove over and pulled Manon into cover under the table.

They narrowly avoided the icicle that avalanched towards them, breaking into tiny little shards scattering across the floor as it hit the tiles. He was about to pull away to go retaliate against the ice spell which had hit the spot where they just had been standing when Manon grabbed his sleeve.

"Furcifer! Jeffrey is dead!"

Furcifer felt like time had slowed down and sped up at that moment. In one instant, all magic spells thrown at one another had been cancelled out as both mages lost their concentration. He could remember Gabrielle's face falling as she heard the news. She had not planned or counted on this.

He had grilled Manon for more information, but all she could tell was that the police had called Russell to inform him about the death and to ask about any family that would need to be informed about this. It wasn't even clear if it had been suicide or natural causes as the body was still under examination and the police were reluctant to give information. A man had been found dead in a police cell. That, obviously, did not reflect well on them.

Gabrielle had fled the scene as soon the news had come. Furcifer suspected she realised any leverage she had was gone and that the news would upset him enough to actually hurt her.

Shoving Manon aside, Gabrielle had rushed out, even leaving her chainmail behind.

Furcifer had not reacted straight away, but had gone and picked up the chainmail, carefully folding it before sitting down now that the lack of magic had shrunk it to its normal size again.

When he considered everything, they had been very civil. Yes, she had used people against him, but this was the first time anyone actually got hurt in their altercation. She was a jilted lover, not a cold blooded murderer. He had seen the shock on her face at that news. It was impossible she had set this in motion.

"NO!" He cried out. "We were- we were supposed to help him, Manon." He said, closing his eyes. "Why-What?"

Manon shook her head. "They didn't say." She sat down near him. "Maybe it was just... Like an aneurysm. People get those."

Furcifer looked up at the bowl with the bangle in it. "No. I did this." He sighed. "I - I deactivated the bracelet. It could have still had an influence and with that falling away..." His voice trailed off. Perhaps a guilt stricken Jeffrey had been unable to live with his crimes once the haze over his mind had passed. All it would have taken was a few minutes, a noose made out of sheets and a distracted guard.

"No!" Manon moved her head to look in his direction. "Stop that. Whatever happened... We all worked in good faith to help him. If he decided to take his own life, that's not our fault. You said he may not even be controlled still - there is no way we should blame ourselves for this!" She let go of the man's face.

"Easy for you to say!" Furcifer bit.

"Easy?" Manon looked over to him incredulously. "Screw you." She simply shook her head. "We were all in this together. We knew things could happen. Twitch did and he still went and did what he needed to do. Aiden risked going back to jail and now we have nothing to show for this effort. So don't play this as if you're the only one feeling anything!" She calmed down, realising she was raising her voice.

"Bloody get dressed and meet me in the classroom. We're ending this." Said Manon, getting up and walking out.

Chapter 30

Russell's eyes were bloodshot and puffy. He'd been talking to both the police and Jeffrey's family in an unending relay. As soon as any information came from one side, he relayed it to the other. It was draining, but it helped him feel like he was at least doing something for his friend and flatmate.

He took a seat in one of the seats and looked around. It had been a while since he had been in one of these. Maybe, if he could save up enough, he could actually go to a proper university when he was done with community college. If Jeffrey had just taught him anything it was the trite but true lesson that life was short. He would rather be poor than to realise he was not doing what he wanted to do.

Aiden walked in and put a hot cocoa in front of him.

"I didn't know if you liked coffee or tea... so I went with hot chocolate." He smiled a little and sat down in the seat in front of him, turning sideways so they could talk. "I have a latte, if you want to trade."

Russell laughed briefly at the nice gesture. "Thanks." He said, looking over to Aiden and sniffing the hot cocoa. "It smells great. I love hot cocoa. Way more than tea or coffee."

"That's good then. How are you doing?"

He shook his head. "Rough. The family's talking to the police but also to me, and the police is also asking me questions." He sighed. "I'll have to go into the station once this little meeting is done, and Jeffrey's father is arriving in town in a few hours." He checked his watch.

"Well, if you need anything, let me know." Aiden briefly touched his hand. "Or if you want to sleep at my place. I know you've been alone at that place for a while, but its different now."

Russell looked up. Aiden... He got it. He seemed to get how he was feeling and why he had been dreading silence or being home alone all day.

"I'd like that." Russell said softly, taking the man's hand and looking up to him. He could see in those eyes that this man had lost someone as well and that he was not just trying to make himself feel better saying that. So far he had been one of the few. Manon had made a few awkward attempts, but the best thing she had been able to do was offer a hug.

"So... do you know why Manon wants us here?" Aiden asked, looking to the front of the classroom.

"Manon called it?" Russell raised an eyebrow. "I just got an email to come here... So I just assumed that was Furcifer."

Furcifer and Manon were the last ones to join in. The mage glanced around, sighing. Jeffrey was gone. Twitch was who knows where. Luckily, everyone else was safe.

"Thank you all for coming." Manon took the lead before Furcifer could open his mouth. "I know it's tough on all of us... But we need to figure out where we're going now. She did not win. Not yet."

"She did." Furcifer leaned back. "She still has Twitch."

Manon blinked. "What?"

"She has him. I asked, she said yes. It kind of went like this: "Hey, Gabrielle, have you seen Twitch?" - "Gosh, yes, I've got him locked away somewhere and you helmets don't know where!"" He took a deep breath. His voice had bellowed through the classroom. He had hardly been aware of raising his voice like that. His nerves were shot after that last magic fight. It had exhausted him, both physically and mentally to fight like that, with magic, a weapon not designed to fight.

Manon sighed. "So what? We go and find him. We know now he didn't leave town on his own free will!" She shrugged. "It's not over."

"It is." Furcifer said. He looked around and wondered how many more of them would get injured or vanish.

"It's too risky. Jeffrey ended up in jail. Manon, you could be expelled and arrested if they found out what you did. Aiden could go back to jail. I'm not risking more of you." Furcifer said, calmer this time.

"That's bullshit." Sighed Manon. "Yes, we could have, we're not. We did it. We just use magic and -"

"That's just it. Magic doesn't make you invincible, Manon." He looked over to her.

"So now what then?" She asked.

"I'm doing what she wants."

Aiden shot up. "No. She will make you destroy all the work you've done for non-mages. She will forbid you to teach to us or even to talk to non-mages."

"So? You will be safe." Furcifer said. "It doesn't matter. It'll just be a small setback."

"Fine." Aiden put his hands up. "Then I'm not talking to you as a mage, but as your friend, Furcifer. There is no way I'm giving up my friend to a coven who will shun anyone non-magical. No matter what I do, Furcifer, they'll make us enemies. Or worse. Please."

"She's let me know she joined the Hopefuls with the Elites. I'm well aware of what you're saying." Furcifer said calmly.

Aiden paled and sat down. "No. You can't join a faction that- Hayden..." He said softly.

Furcifer sighed. "They looked into your wife's death. It was not one of theirs. And I would be in the Elites, not with the witches." He knew this was bad - Aiden hardly ever used the name of his late wife.

"You shut up!" Aiden cried loudly, looking over to him. "You know it was witches and that they helped cover it up so it would look better on the magic community. They killed her because I was showing off, and because killing her would hurt me more than dying myself. And if you buy into that coven thing, if you join a faction, you will only strengthen that idea. You will strengthen those ideals"

"They don't kill mages." Furcifer tried to reason. "That's why-"

"That's why it was okay for them to kill my human wife?!" He took a deep breath, a fireball growing within his hands. "If you do this, Atze Furcifer, I will never, ever forgive you. You will no longer be a friend of mine."

"So be it then. I'd rather save the lives of actual people than to uphold the memory of one dead one!" Furcifer called out.

"Alright." Aiden said. "You have made your choice." He grabbed his messenger bag. As he left he looked over to Russell. "Sorry."

Furcifer closed his eyes. At least they would be safe.

Russell looked torn between hearing the rest and going after Aiden. After looking down at the cup of hot cocoa, he made his decision.

"Aiden, wait!" He rushed out after the man, hoping he could catch him before he teleported away or something.

Manon sighed. The door closed behind Russell as she looked over to Furcifer.

"Is there... Any guarantee they will let Twitch go if you join?"

"No, but I would be able to set him free myself." Furcifer at least hoped so. His hopes were set on that at least. It was heart-breaking to lose Aiden as a friend but he could save Twitch and hope the young mage would not hate him.

He walked out of the auditorium, pausing on the doorstep. First things first he would need to find Gabrielle and tell her of his... decision. He walked up to his tower and packed the basics of his belongings, leaving as much as he could. Whatever he left, others could use. Really all he took was his identity documents, phone and clothes. Everything else could be replaced, and honestly, would probably be provided by the faction. After glancing over his room, he closed the door and walked out.

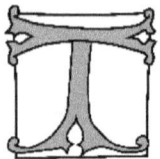

Chapter 31

Twitch had cleaned the flat, which took him to around noon. In order to not go insane being alone, he had a strict regimen that kept him busy from moment to moment. He had grown used to the heat of cooking enough again that he could cook, which meant cooking a meal took up another hour of his day. And so, from hour to hour, he could keep himself occupied a full day and sleep well.

Of course it was boring, but he was trying to survive. There were few books to read and fewer people to talk to. All in all he was being a model prisoner here and he hoped that if he showed he was cooperative, they would soon let him out of here.

Let's see- today he was going to make a pasta dish from scratch. It would take a bit longer than an hour, but that was good. He was taking out the ingredients for the pasta dough when he heard a sound from the door, a soft knock.

"Mary?" He perked up, wiping some flour off of his hands as he walked to the door.

The door opened. For a second Twitch considered pushing past the young woman. However, seeing how serious she looked, he decided not to and even took a step back.

Mary closed the door behind her.

"Hi Twitch. I'm afraid I have some bad news. Jeffrey... was found dead in his cell. We don't know much. But Furcifer stole the bangle so... I'm guessing it's because he broke the connection with Gabrielle. I think... I think he killed himself. I'm sorry." She was happy to blame the death on Furcifer, which made Twitch curl hands into fists.

"You don't get to say that!" He cried out. "You - you would blame it on Furcifer, you useless piece of-" He gasped.

"Who just- you turned your back on him, and me!" He felt the heat gathering into the palms of his hands and closed his eyes.

Shit, shit, shit. He needed to calm down. But at the same time... The last time he had been this angry, he had actually managed to do things he usually could never bring himself to do. It seemed his mind had formed a strong relation to fire magic, which he usually too afraid to use.

Feed it, he thought to himself. Think what they did to you. To Manon. To Jeffrey. Fight for them.

He opened his eyes again and looked at the woman.

"Get out of my way, Mary. I'm not asking you twice." He pushed past her and grabbed the doorknob. The pure heat emanating from his hands melted the insides of the lock until he could just tear open the door. As he walked out he touched the walls, leaving a trace of burned paint and tearing pipes, bursting open from the heat forced through them. Slowly, the heat on his hands turned into fire, but he felt no fear as the walls around him caught fire. Memories of Jeffrey flooded his brain. That innocent, stupid little boy being used as a pawn. Manon's fear when she realised the bracelet was actually controlling her. His own fear when Gabrielle used his greatest fear against him. Mary, standing there and watching, little more than a year after she had sworn to protect all members of the Hopefuls.

This had happened only once since he had been burned. Perhaps it was the emotional link with that moment, but strong emotion made him excel at fire magic. Fear usually held him back from using it, as it had the last time. He had freaked out seeing a fireball appear. He had quickly put it out and calmed himself.

This time he would use it to tear this place down. He slowly made his way towards the stairs. From what he could see he was near the top floor, so he had a way to go. He was not going to see Gabrielle. Even with this momentary power he did not want to take her on. He had no desire to hurt anyone. More than anything, he wanted to take down the entire building and deal a blow to Gabrielle without killing a single person.

As he walked down the stairs he took small detours into the halls to start the fire alarms, making sure everyone had time to get out. By the time he reached the ground floor, he had seen every single mage he knew storming past him. Some had given him frightened looks. One or two had begged him to tell them what was going on, but had burned themselves trying to take a hold of him... He had just ignored them and pushed past. Smoke was filling up the hallways and the smell of fire was everywhere.

On the bottom floor, he started on a long, complicated spell. The fire in his hands was now consuming his lower arms but he didn't even feel it. He ended the spell sending several fireballs upward, melting their way through the floors and causing everything they touched to light up in flames. The heat emanating off of him made his hair wave. Later, a mage who had witnessed everything, would swear she had seen his eyes light up eerily, and smoke coming out of his mouth as he opened it. Even under his skin fire seemed to pulse rather than blood.

Soon, the entire building would be lit up, up to and including the penthouse. He doubted anyone would be killed– every mage knew enough magic to get out safely or owned some commuting beads. But the tower of flats, the pride of the Hopefuls, would be gone. And they would be hard pressed to find another building like this. He smiled to himself as he saw another few mages rush out. He had not stooped as low as them and he was proud of himself for that. With a little smile, he walked out of the building as the fire he was carrying in his arms went out.

Chapter 32

Gabrielle frowned at the notification which had almost made her phone vibrate off of the small coffee shop table. The Hopeful building had gone up in flames.

Oh well. Good thing she had not been there for that. All that mattered was that they had helped her reach her goal. She did not need them anymore and it turned out that Twitch had been the perfect time bomb. The destruction of the building would mean the Elite and the Hopefuls would be eager to expel Twitch, and without his clan, he was nothing. He was a pack animal, who cared for others too much to take care of himself. On his own he wouldn't last long. Meanwhile, the destruction of the Hopefuls' building meant they would be more than eager to join the Elite or move to the Scribes.

-Be safe, Mary. Go to the Elites and take any Hopefuls you can- She texted. -While I'm out you're in command-

She put the phone away as Furcifer entered the coffee shop and put down the folded up chainmail in front of her.

"You clean up nicely." Furcifer said.

"I just changed clothes. Much like you. And thank you, that was an expensive top." She shrugged. "I preferred the towel, though." She joked as she put the chainmail into her purse.

"You can't flirt at a time like this." Furcifer sat down and looked over the menu. "I'm coming with you. Just... stop all this. Don't harm Twitch. Don't touch my students."

"Deal. Twitch has already been released." She was technically not lying. "I knew you would come crawling to me as soon as your plans failed." She sat back. "The espresso con panna is amazing in this place. They make it with coffee flavoured whipped cream."

"Yeah, I'll get a double one of those." He said to the waitress, who waited for Gabrielle's order before vanishing.

"I promise, the rest of your humans are safe. Nothing will happen." She nodded.

Furcifer took a deep breath. "So... congratulations. You won."

"Oh don't be so dour, Atze! It'll be fun!" She patted his cheek. "You'll be an Elite, working with the best to research magic, and you won't have to worry about a single thing. That's your dream, isn't it?" She smiled and looked over. "You will be so happy."

Furcifer looked over. "And what if I am not?"

"I will make you happy." She leaned in and took his hands. "I do love you still, Atze." She said, looking up into his eyes.

He sighed and closed his eyes. "Alright then. When do we start?"

"Soon! But there's always time for coffee, first. After that, we walk out of here. Together." She smiled brightly.

Epilogue

Furcifer often wondered afterwards if he had made the right decision that day. But whenever his mind tended to wander, he found another problem to keep himself occupied. He would think of Twitch, who was missing but alive – he would leave little clues from time to time. A sneaky photobomb in a photo of a magic related article. A little package with sloppy writing containing a magical item he had found on his travels. Furcifer could live with that and hoped Twitch had been able to make his peace with all that had happened.

Aiden had taken over the magic lessons, much against his will. From the postcard he had received of Aiden he had learned that he and Russell were dating.

He wondered how that would work out if the man decided to go to university, which Aiden had hinted at before.

Manon was still helping out Aiden as a teaching assistant, though she was in her last year now herself, pursuing a master's degree in magic. Because of the lack of a well-specified program, she had to fight to make it work. Knowing Manon and Aiden though, he knew those two could work it out.

Furcifer looked out of the window of the tower. He was now head of the Elites, while Gabrielle had become head of the Hopefuls. And every day, their knowledge grew.

The story continues in

Asa's Blessing

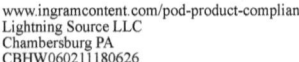